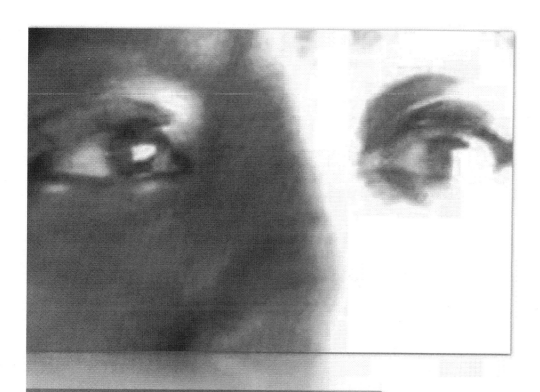

WHY SHOULDN'T I?

A REFLECTION ON BLACK MOTHERHOOD

"My thoughts and questions about life, parenting and other crazy stuff!!"

By Willie Esther Curtis Williams

The real life question I often asked myself while raising two generations of young black men as a single parent with no instructions, warranties, guarantees, rebates or exchanges! Definitely no money back!!

With Love, Ms Willie E.

Dedication

This book is dedicated to my children, my grandchildren, my siblings, my parents, my family and all the wonderful people who made me smile. Here's to you.

"Family   faces
are.......mirrors.   People
that belong to us, we see
the   past,   present   and
future."

Gail   Lumet   Buckley,
1937-

Author

Mr. Richard W. Curtis, Jr.
02/1925 (POPS) 08/2009

My Daddy

Welcome to our world......

And we all survived!

Table of Contents

Introduction

My Victory Laps

Why Shouldn't I

Introduction

Why Shouldn't I is the title of my book that describes the life and experiences that I encounter while raising three children as a single mother and four boys as a single grandmother. In other words, my life's experiences and lessons as a parent that I want to share with other parents because I want you to know that you are not all by yourself in this straight on the job training experience. There is no policy or procedure manual. Talking about trial and error, this is part of my jurney in full force.

My life is an interesting story, trust me. This book should bring laughter, tears, joy, strength and courage through all kinds of life changing situations. As a parent I proved that you can overcome just about any obstacle that you encounter if you believe in yourself, your support group, the people you surround yourself with and most of all, as you believe in God you know all things are possible no matter what it look like.

Now before we get started down this road to reading, I got a question for you, do you want to read about parenting, teenage pregnancy, domestic violence, being a gunshot victim, #metoo moment, a boyfriend who was married, relocating, dating and finding an abandoned newly born baby? If so you are in the right book, but if you're not interested in these things all I can say is I guess it is your loss. I say this for the simple reason that if you would just sit back and take this journey with me you will find it to be an enjoyable book for you to read, you might even find yourself or some similarity, so come on, sit back, kick back and lets go for it. Don't lose out on some good reading, take a chance on me. I survived through parenting two generations as a single black momma and grandmomma, I know I can tell you something, trust me. Give me a little of your time for you to see I am about what I say I am about.

Chapter 1. Who is Ms. Willie Esther Curtis Williams?

The making of me....

Who is Willie Esther Curtis Williams?

Chapter1. Who is Willie Esther Curtis Williams?

Who am I? Let's begin this time that we are going to spend together learning about me with a proper introduction and a little bit about me. Here goes, my name is Willie Esther Curtis Williams. I was born Willie Esther Curtis, February 28th, 1958 at Cook County Hospital in Chicago, Illinois. I was born unto Richard Willie Curtis Jr. and Kizzieanna White. Descendants of Wilmon White (maternal grandfather) and Richard W. Curtis Sr (paternal grandfather). Never met my grandmothers, both were deceased before I was born. I am a high-school graduate of Emerson High School, Gary IN and a four year graduate from Purdue University Calumet, Hammond IN majoring in communications with criminology as my minor. This is one of my best accomplishments because with all the twists and tangles in my life it took me eleven years to EARN this four year degree. I am proud of myself for finishing school cause that shit wasn't easy.

I am the mother of three and the grandmother of six I have two sons living and well, one daughter deceased at the age of 28. She had four sons when she passed away. Their ages were 3,4,7, and 12. I also have a grandson and granddaughter by my youngest son. I have a whole bunch of sons and daughters that I did not birth into this world but they are an important part of my life, they call me Mama or Mama Willie. Otherwise I am known as Miss Willie. I have 7 brothers and 3 sisters. Two brothers of whom are deceased and one that has been missing since 2009. The other 4 brothers are living and well. My sisters and I are all 7 years apart, my oldest sister is 7 years older than me I am 7 years older than my younger sister, interesting isn't it? Never a dull moment or holiday in our house, because we would not allow it.

About this time in my life, I want you to know, our family had a lot of men. They were always wanting to tell you something about life, what they used to do, and when they did it. To me that was a good thing because I learned a lot from them about men. They wanted me to know the real deal about life, family, money and most of all growing up, so therefore I am what I would call me well experienced in the area of black men and the family. I've been around a lot of them to know about the black man, how he acts, what he likes, is he smart, at least so I thought I knew, they change everyday, all day. Yep, unpredictable black men is and was my life as you read about my many episodes in this book.

I was raised by my dad, both parents' fathers, great uncles, pastors and neighbors. Some of the neighborhood men weren't worth discussing, however we did have some male neighborhood fathers who took care of their large families as well as the neighborhood kids. These fathers ruled the community and did not take no prisoners. Back in the day this was how the village worked, neighbors were the eyes and ears of your parents when they were not around. They kicked your butt if you was or they thought you was out of pocket and nothing was said but another ass whooping from your parents. A double whammy in other words.

I was born in the era where what 8 to 10 kids was the minimum amount of children in a family. With a family of 10 children my father was present where he ruled his house with an iron hand, made all the decisions (so he thought, momma made them) and was the main provider for the family. I was a daddy's girl, as a matter of fact he called me his "Golden Child" because he said everything I touch turns to gold. He said I would never fail at anything I tried to do. He was my joy, my inspiration I loved my dad so much because he loved me unconditionally. We had a great father daughter relationship. It really hurt me and the rest of the family when he lost his eyesight before my daughter was born. As a matter of fact he never saw any grandchild born after 1976. Even with him being blind he still was the head honcho. Nothing changed. He still was my dad, who "paid the cost to be the boss." He just could not see. My mom on the other hand was a force to be reckoned with. Sometimes I really wondered if she even liked me. There were times I questioned her love for me. I even have had therapy sessions about our mother daughter relationship, but nonetheless she is the force behind me becoming the great business woman I am. I have the ability to relate to people, to try understand some of them in an effective manner. She stood strong in teaching me to know that God is real in my life and to trust Him always. All those teachings, being active in church, including Christmas, Easter, Mother's Day, Father's Day, Church Anniversary, Black History, Woman in Red and other event that needed speeches, I was it. Those teachings, evenings and mornings spent cleaning up the church or just being there every time the church door was open was important because it's a big part of what built my character. Thanks Mom. I didn't understand it then but I understand it now and if it hadn't been for those moments that you made me stay there, persevere land learn despite all my complaining and hiding, I wouldn't be a jack of all trades and a master of none as a I am right now.

I have to take a few pages and give my mom a lot of love and high fives for without her I would not be here. She did good.

One thing for sure, every time you saw my mom she was working on something, creating something, cooking something or just making something happen. That was the type of woman she was. She was always there with the family house door opening it for someone in need or some family member who needed a roof over their head. That was Mom. Now that she's grown into her eighties and had a stroke, she is unable to move effectively like she what used to. It's kind of hard seeing her like that but I know what character of woman she was and still is. She did not let anything grow under her feet she did not let any news slip by her, she knew everything about everybody and now it's so different for her and us, as a matter fact, I believe it's really hard on her but thank God she still here in the land of the living. She had a bout with cancer in 1968 what she was given one year to live. She was a young mother with a 5 month old baby and 9 small children. I think I was 10 or 11 when I had the responsibility to step up to the plate and assist with the younger brothers and sister. I had older sister who had other ideas about life, returned home to help me and mom to take care of us. Thank God she came home, I really missed and needed her. I loved her so much and because she was the eldest she was like our second mom. She was one I had the late night sister talks with. My beautiful younger sister was three, so we could not really talk about much. I also had an older brother who was diagnosed with sickle cell anemia who required attention as well as a lot of medical care. The responsibilities that I took on an early age because Dad had to work were huge, we had to depend upon ourselves for getting ready for school, doing our homework, doing our chores without adult supervision sometimes. We were young children with a big burden. My great-aunts, the older ladies in the family, bless their hearts were wonderful, loving and caring. One great-aunt, and my beautiful aunt on my mother's side were the ones who prepared meals and came to visit us make sure that we had what we needed when Mama was sick or in the hospital. I had another great aunt who sewed and repaired our torn or worn clothes and furniture. Aunties are so important and valuable.

Momma eventually came home but was still very weak as she tried to take care of her children. It was a slow process but we did whatever we could do to help her. Home was a small 3 bedroom 1 bathroom house with 8 children and two parents. We managed somehow. In that small space we had a living room, kitchen, storage room, a big backyard and plenty of love. I was raised by two parents, a father who worked and took care of the bills and take care of the house and a mother who worked until she couldn't to assist Daddy who was doing his best at keeping us comfortable, mama was still sick and sometimes bedridden. She kept saying all she wanted was a place to put her children where they will be comfortable and together if and when she passed.

Soon she started seeking God more and more each day. She began to attend church services and all kinds of meetings, church services, prayer meetings, anything dealing with learning about God. Mind you she was 34 years old maybe 35 woman, with a house full of babies, a husband that drank a lot and she was sick unto death. She needed something in her life. She chose God. She began to go to this one church, Prayer House of Faith, Gary IN and that was the beginning of a change in her life, there was a pep in her step a smile on her face. Since she had found God she has started moving around a little bit more, just a little bit more. She still wanted and prayed for a bigger house and better house for her children. She was determined and trusted God for an answer to her prayers.

My dad's younger brother used to work on old houses and he found my family a house, it was a fixer upper and told Mama and Daddy all they needed to pay was the closing cost and the house was theirs. They did not have the money for that and still somehow we got that four bedroom 2 bathroom house with a garage! We moved from a 5 room flat house to a 9 room two story home with an unfinished spooky basement. Talk about an upgrade! The house was located in the downtown area so that means that there was a diverse population. Our new neighbors were from all different walks of life. Family life was important, cherished and respected.

School days

The new school was not too far from where we live so walking to and from school daily was not going to be a problem, besides the neighbor had a lot of kids so I thought I would have new friends.

The time was October 1968 and Civil Rights has come into effect and so the country was in a different cultural flavor. At this time they were experimenting in the education system as far as integrating the schools. Lucky us. We were part of the integration process into Emerson High School and they started by bringing the 6th graders into a high school. The school now began from 6 to 12 grade and they had a plan all the 6th grade students would remain on the ground floor. We were not allowed upstairs at any time, we had our own floor in the school. There were six graders that were bussed from the housing projects and the urban city neighborhoods to predominantly white school. We had never seen that many white people together at one time except for on TV and in the movies. Me being a dark skin skinny black girl with big thick glasses and short unkempt hair was not the favorite student in the school. I found myself being the object of bullying. I was always being the center of conversation of vicious verbal attacks about my appearance, not to mention that my name was Willie so there was a lot of days I cried from the viciousness of the students who had no idea of what my home environment was. They didn't know I had seven brothers, one who stayed in and out of the hospital, two sisters, and a terminally ill mother. They didn't know that I had a father who drank a lot, who was struggling to take make ends meet, take care of the his large family and continue to be a support for his sick wife. They didn't know that I was a caretaker of all those children. They had no idea I had a brother at home that was diagnosed with sickle cell anemia and stayed sick all the time. They just didn't know or care, but due to their ignorance they persisted and continued to make me cry feel bad and most of all have the lowest self-esteem that you could possibly imagine. Talk about feeling like nothing and managing to still forge forward takes a lot of strength and I did it. As time goes by I make a few friends because they found out how smart I was. They were so busy judging a book by its cover, they didn't even realize that I could help them out with their studies or I was a friend that they needed for my smarts or I that was a good person who had feelings and needed friends too.

I somehow managed to finish the 6th grade and moved on to the 7th at the same school with the same people and they were doing the same thing. Another year of this madness, this time the madness had spread to the block where I lived! They begin leaving notes on our front stairs, talking about the poorest family in town. They would leave pots, soap all kinds of stuff on our stairs and it was one or some of our neighbors! We could not imagine which one it was. But now as well as getting bullied in school I was getting bullied at home by the neighbors! This went on for some time and my father finally put a stop to it because he started addressing all the neighbors and telling them whoever it is they better stop or he's going to be planted out there at night and shoot whoever is on his stairs! Yeah they were so bold they were still leaving the notes at front door then then this note came about two days after he let them know he would shoot them. It said "I like Willie Esther Curtis even if she's the poorest girl in town." No more notes came after that. The neighborhood got a little better. The boys stopped snickering at me so much because at that time I began to develop. So now they knew that I was really a girl because my body began to really develop and guess you could say that I had a nice shape for a teen aged girl. I made it through that year. I learned and decided that what they said about me couldn't affect my intellect. I am succeeding.

The years go by at Emerson high school and I am now a high school student and the bullying toned down. They stopped a lot with the comments and I was now grooming myself a little better and getting a little at ease with school. Now enters the school a girl about 5 feet 11 inches with big bubble eyes and a mole on one of those eyes. I don't know which one it was and did not care, but it was for sure was going to bully me and bully me and bully me. I don't even know her or why she chose me! She wasn't the best looking thing as a matter of fact you say she was downright skinny and funny looking but with my low self-esteem self I allowed her to bully me and make me feel even worse than she looked. I remember one of my most humiliating experience in my high school years was what she did to me was in the middle of the hallway when the bell rang at the end of the school day. The hallway was always crowded because it was a big school, the bell had just rang for the end of the day, so the hallway was really busy. She ran up behind me and pulled my wig off, threw it to the floor running away laughing with all or a majority of all students congregating on the main floor! My wig was on the floor, my hair was short. Everybody was just laughing and pointing! I was so embarrassed and angry that I picked my new Freedom Curl wig up, put it back on and with tears in my eyes took off after her in the direction she headed and could not catch nor find her. My few friends told me not to fight her because they didn't want me to get in trouble. They knew in the angry state that was in, there was going to be a real fight! This time no backing down! You see under that wig I had not combed my short nappy hair and it looked terrible, somewhat like a carpet, lint balls and all! She deserves an ass whooping for this move! I let it go for then, but I did tell one girl who's supposed to be my friend that I was going to whoop this girl's ass one day. She went back and told my arch enemy what I said. What a pal. As the days rolled on after the incident, I was eating lunch in the cafeteria with a couple of so called friends, the crowded cafeteria let me remind you, my nemesis enters and confronts me loudly saying " Willie Esther I heard you said you was going to whup my ass. Well here it is!" She turned around and slapped the area where ass supposed to be. She was inviting me to her ass! I was eating or trying to eat this nasty tuna salad, picking through it with my head down, never looking up. She humiliated me again! Why won't she stop I am thinking to myself! Everybody in the cafeteria was looking at me and how she was talking to me and berating me, their eyes and ears wide open waiting to see what is gonna happen next. I had had enough! Whatever my consequences was going to be it was going to be, so I picked that bowl of tuna salad up and smashed it in her face twisting the bowl so it would smush in her face! Tuna fish face! Ha-ha! This time the attention and laughter was on her as she ran out of the cafeteria humiliated! Wow Willie Esther Curtis you stood up for yourself. I thought to myself, why shouldn't I?

I continued my journey of education in the same school and I still had some haters and people who wanted to talk about me but I felt just a little stronger. I just let shit roll off of me now. I began to get involved in school activities. I was part of the track team, I tried out for cheerleading, I was a member of the marching band for 5 years, Future Homemakers of America, Girls Athletic Association and any other school activity that I could be a part of. I was trying to enjoy school and the people.

A vast majority of my teachers were white and what I called old at the time. They liked me because I was smart and a good student. I finished my studies and I graduated in the top half of my class and I had only one secret, I was pregnant when I graduated and nobody knew or so I thought. It seemed that my great aunt was sitting beside my mom and dad at my graduation. She told them, "Something wrong with her, her face just don't look right!" This statement turned my parents into the PBI, the Parents Bureau of Investigations, hell they were worse than the FBI! Question after question! I knew all the answers but I did not answer. I stood firmly on the 5th Amendment in my mind. I was scared as hell, I ain't saying nuthin! You open your mouth and tell them you are going to die! I stood firm on not answering a question. They realized they were not getting anywhere with me so they sent me to the doctor and his tests said I was pregnant. I already knew and was hoping the pregnancy magically disappeared by this office visit, but it didn't. When I shared the news about the baby for the first time in my life I saw my father cry. I cried again too. We were crying for 2 different reasons.

I had not accepted the whole notion of being pregnant. I did not want to be pregnant nor did i want to be a mom and wanted as few people as possible to know my soon to be huge secret so I stayed away from everybody. My room was my safe haven. My family rarely saw me. I got as invisible as I could with a belly. I really accepted that I was pregnant when I was 5 months into it when I had to tell my parents that I felt something move inside of me. I was so scared. I had just finished high school 2 month ago and was headed to the United States Air Force but my physical examination again much to my denial revealed that I was pregnant so that killed the thought of me going anywhere. I had to forget the fact that I was also accepted into Ball State University too. My education and career was now motherhood. I cried again. I just wanted to run away from all of this crazy "having a baby madness" but I could not. I was a scared pregnant teenager not knowing what to expect.

So now I have finally accepted the fact that there's going to be another life that I am about bring into this world regardless of the circumstances . I gotta to take care of this little darling for the rest of his/her life and my life too. This was a heartbreaking blow to my dad, because his Golden Child is now with child and not talking about marriage or the baby daddy. Quite a big blow to my mom too. They would have another mouth to feed. I had no income. I don't even know where the first bag of diapers was coming from. How do I feed the baby? How do you take care of a baby? I had no idea what I was in store for me, but I knew that this was my body and I shared it daily with this individual for nine months and that something was going to happen and I was going to have to get and be ready.   As I grew into the pregnancy and felt the baby moving, I began to anticipate and await the new arrival of a mini me. On this particular day I get this excruciating pain in my back that I cannot explain.   My dad is at work in Chicago, my mom is in the bed sleep and my back is killing me, literally killing me. What the hell is this? This pain is making me stop and stand still. So I go downstairs and I lay down next to my mom and I tell her my back is really hurting and she says "are you having that baby?" I dunno I have never had a baby before. I have no idea what is going on, I thought to myself but I dare not answer her like that either. She gets up, gets dressed and takes me to the hospital. When we get me checked in I'm dilated to 2 cm. What does that mean? I am an 18 year old girl, scared half way out of her mind, body acting crazy and about to have a baby.   Just to describe the pain, I was experiencing, I must describe it as indescribable.   You could not melt me down and pour me on somebody I hated and wanted dead and not wish that kind of pain on them. This pain was some shit for my ass! Somewhere close to the end of the labor I passed out, went to sleep or they put me to sleep. I think they put me to sleep because I keep banging my head against the bed repeatedly. The doctor asked, "Is she having a seizure?" I answered the doctor for them, "no I'm trying to knock myself out you're not doing it!" They eventually gave me something or I knocked myself out, I don't know. When I awoke I had given birth to my beautiful baby girl and what I woke up to is a whole nother story. Just to give you some idea, I woke up next to the girl who bullied me all through high school! I spoke of our last tuna salad encounter previously in this book, so we just going to leave that there. But every time I think about waking up to the voice of my school nemesis, the girl who made my life a living hell for a long time, the girl I wish would have fallen in a well full of old cow piss and manure and just be stinky forever, is having a baby the same day I did! I could just scream! Tell me God don't have a serious sense of humor! After being transferred in to my room, (thank God she was not one of my roommates!), I told my hospital roommates, who happened to be older ladies, what happened between us during our school days and they kept her away from me during my 4 day stay. For once I knew what protection felt like and it felt so good.

In the span of the next 10 years or so I had two more children, two sons as a matter of fact one son is 7 years younger than my daughter and the other son is 10 years younger than my daughter. I even got married which lasted not long physically but legally, a few decades. I will always have love for him in my heart. He married a damaged woman with two children and tried to love her the best he knew how as a damaged man. Then we got pregnant! I was able to conceive and I birthed my last son as a married woman. The best gift from that marriage was our son. This beautiful gift could not keep us together as husband and wife even tho we tried.

I went on and finished my college education, taught school for 10 years, started my own education and training company for mothers who were participants in our socio-economic system. Which by the way has an 85% success rate! The best reason for the success rate is because I once was a participant in the state assistance program, welfare as we know it so I could relate to them and their situations of financial, physical and mental survival with children.

Then and when I relocated to Omaha, I began working with families, schools and community organizations for the academic, social and emotional success of children. I also founded a community parent organization. It came into existence because as well as myself there were two other mothers who were wanting their children to succeed and were having struggles with the school system. We got others to join and we were well on our way. Other parents joined us and we were a hot item because all parents wanted was someone to care and advocate for them and their children. We did just that and we also tried to empower parents to have an active voice as far as educational decisions of their child. We took them to our Parent Academy which was created, and implemented by myself, other parents, community members, businesses and organizations. We were a successful part of a family recovery initiative that was funded by President Barrack Obama's American Reinvestment and Recovery Act Stimulus dollars. Omaha Public schools was on board. We were a wraparound service which had resources, training programs, classes and events. We did the damn thang! Included in the initiative, parents had information taught and given to them information including their rights and how to communicate with their school district to encourage them to work together peacefully and productively for the success of their child. At least that is what tried to do. Sometimes it worked, sometime it didn't. They were equipped with information and they knew that had rights in their child's education they were now more vocal and somehow this wasn't popular with some members of the school district and school administrations. I wonder why?

Through the years I was well trained through the National Title I Parent Chapter of Elementary and Secondary Education Act of 1965 so I was able to guide and educate families, schools and communities on Title I law and I tried my best to pass this knowledge on. I have travelled all over the country learning and being trained about families and education. I have met Secretaries of Education, lawmakers, people who hold positions in the arena of education. Families, Schools and Communities capacity building, training and education are my areas of expertise. I was even invited and flown to Washington D.C. to sit with the nation's top education decision makers to give my input to help formulate a strategic systemic plan for families, school and communities to better assist our children. They believed in me.

As far as my thoughts about me, I consider myself a people's person who paves the way for others to shine. A trailblazer. I am behind the scenes a lot watching everything fall into place. Sometimes you see me, sometimes you don't. I don't have to be seen to be effective. My belief is that everybody has some type of gifting. How you use it is up to you. I try to use my gift to benefit others.

Chapter 2. My Thoughts about Parenting.

When they told me about life, they should have made me listen.

Chapter 2. My Thoughts About Parenting

Being a parent was my choice and a decision that I made to bring another life into this world and to love unconditionally until they leave this world and even after. So however a situation or outcome may be or turn out concerning them, I have to deal with it because I made that choice to be a mother whether I like it or not.

Let's start with me and my trial and error parenting skills. Some worked some didn't, but still I had to try. I had to find a way to teach my fellas life lessons about life events, the one lesson that summed it all was survival. There are so many branches to the tree of survival and I found one in particular I felt they needed and was focused on it a lot. As I taught my children about life, one thing that I realized as a parent that one day they would have to live without me, so teaching them survival and how to get along without me is a must. This might sound cryptic or strange but it's the truth. If they lean and depend on me all the time and I do the thinking for them I am doing them a great disservice. I must teach my fellas how to think for themselves no matter how strange the lesson or unorthodox the method, as long as they are living breathing and functioning afterwards they are ok. Life's lessons are not always pleasant or pretty. As long as they learned was my satisfaction point, that was all I wanted no matter what route I had to take, I did not care whether they liked me or not. They was gonna learn and survive in this cold hearted world.

There were boundaries I taught too. There must be teaching of respect of others and self-respect, also self-control and self-discipline. They don't learn these wonderful skills and values all at one time or overnight. It takes time. Sometimes they act like they only learned one or possibly two of these skills, that's when my job as a parent comes in and make sure that the lessons that I am teaching them is learned and learned well because these are what they will take forward to their children and their children and their children's grandchildren. In other words my legacy. What is it that I want my generations to remember about me and my Crazy Action Plans, oops I mean my lessons?

I'm not saying as a parent I am perfect or I had my shit together at all times and I'm not saying all my message were correct, but my intentions we're headed in the right direction. My intentions were to keep my kid safe, alive and for him to be able to survive as a black man in this society. I guess sometimes I should have called Child Protective Services on myself for some of my reactions that the boys made me put them through that required drastic measures. I Thank God I did not own any guns, spears or special weapons because this may have been a totally different story. This book would have been written and published from the local or state jail or maybe even prison! But by the Grace of God we made it through and everybody is still in one piece physically, I am not commenting on their mental status! They survived and so did I. No jail time. No probation. No hospitalizations. Look at God!

Emotionally these fellas and their feelings are something else! I don't even know where or how to begin to describe these fella's emotions, they can split and go into all types of directions and feelings that exist in the atmosphere in a hot second. And without any notice or possible sign! One minute they love me, the next thing I know they have turned on me! The kid, my kid, just did an about face on everything, got defiant and did something I warned them not to do and then get an attitude about it. Yep boys get emotional and crazy too! Almost like they have PMS! I be trying to come to grips with the ever-changing environments of parenting without suicide, homicide or genocide. I think to myself, "wonder how many years I will get if I....?"as I call my attorney friend to discuss my concerns of how or what kinda charge and much time I would get if I committed the deed I was thinking. She would inform me even tho we were" girls" that she would have to testify against me because it was premeditated because I told her what I was planning or going to do. She straight up told me that my option was not a good option for our friendship either. Now I gotta try and figure out another approach because I love her and our friendship, I gotta come up with another plan. Damn! With this new plan I got to try to keep my sanity, my freedom and our friendship. Decisions. Decisions. One thing I know is that I won't tell her ass the next time! Since she said violence ain't the answer all the time, I will have to defer to my Crazy Action Plan handbook. I feel every parent needs a plan of action that requires a plan of action. The reason I say that is because there comes a time when it would be smooth sailing for a while in my life and home, but just when I thought that I had a situation all under control, handled all well and things were going handy dandy, Bam! Boom! Ping! That one little thing that had a slither of a chance, it could have been anything, that one little disruption that I thought I handled, rears its ugly face. My whole world feeling of well-being and contentment is in chaos. Then this kid comes from nowhere and blindsides me with some bullshit. I mean you think you got things going on to a point where you can exhale. Then the gut punch! We are not talking physical but rather a mental and emotional blow that has the same reaction as if it were beat up by a mob. He has created a problem within the problem of the problem that you thought was no longer a problem! Real shit right here, he got me and him standing before the peoples with the situation in question being questioned and then he tells you he sorry but he don't know what happened. You don't know what what? His ass got me out here looking like this and that is the best he got? He got selectively spontaneous amnesia all of a sudden? That's what happened! He either lost his memory or his damned mind! Whatever happened he better make it unhappen! God I pray You intervene for him right here, right now, right fast! My sanity light is real dim right now and fading fast!

Being blindsided by your kid is a feeling of helplessness, betrayal with so many emotions mixed up in it. You don't know what to feel. I am now thinking to myself and convincing myself that I still have to learn and love this kid who disturbed my few moments of sanity and messed with my chi with this drummed up memory lapse. I have to somehow remind myself after self-medicating that parenting is a choice and I chose this path. He got me messed up, again! "Cool out," I say to myself and "cool out now!" I don't wanna cool out right now, I wanna destroy him! "Talking to yourself is fine, makes you feel so much better" Thank you Earth Wind and Fire for this song! I had to sing this song to myself a couple hundred times with this bunch of fellas, and say to myself a couple thousand times "this is the path I chose. This is my decision. Please try to stay out of police custody. Parenting ain't easy!"

In one of the abundant conversations I had with me, myself and I after one of many disciplinary incidents in our humble abode was "Importantly girl learn not to physically discipline your children while you are angry 'cause you could seriously hurt your kid and or you could get yourself in a world of trouble. No matter how mad you get you must stop and think and get him later. I know this is some hard shit to do. But you have to. It cost you too much if you don't. " Yup this is what I told myself. Since violence ain't the answer for this situation, what we have now is a situation within a situation. Deal with it. Try to figure out a solution without jail or death being the outcome. Think. Then you think about what the hell he did and you back at square one, because you want to cause something to happen to him by you and not in the kid's favor! Stop and think. That is some hilarious serious shit to think to yourself when your kid has made you mad enough to want to............

Again I had to tell myself another couple hundred times this is the path I chose, this is my decision, no matter how mad I get I must stop and think about it and get that ass later. I know this is some hard shit to do. But I had to.   My fellas have made me so mad that if I even moved physically the next move most definitely would not be what they wanted. So I try to remain stationary in one spot, away from the child, cause if I move……..I ain't responsible. At that point I need adult supervision. Prime example, I was visiting my mother who lived on the next street from me, I telephoned my son who lives at home with me to come over because I wanted him to do something. 10 minutes went by no son. I called again he said he was coming. 10 minutes went by again, no son, by this time I am furious! Smoke was coming out of both of my ears, I was spitting fire and walking fast. I hate to wait on my children, if I ask them to do something they should not make me wait! I finally walked home and by the time I got in the housee I was seeing red. Thinking real loud to myself, there is going to be a misunderstanding on sight when I see this boy! My nephews and my sons were upstairs playing a video game and as I was coming in the door my son was coming down the stairs. Before I realized it my anger took over my actions and I grabbed my son and slammed him into the wall, and asked him "didn't I tell you to come here? Why are you making me wait on you?" This kid is about 5'11 or 6 ft tall. I had him by his collar and when I slammed him against the wall again, he went through it! I was that angry! I did not realize the strength I had at that moment. He was literally sitting in the wall with a puzzled look on his face similar to a deer in headlights. All of his cousins that was visiting heard the racket came running down maybe to about 5 stairs where they could see what was going on.   They saw him sitting in the wall and me standing in front of him, they turned around swiftly, smartly thinking to themselves we not going to be involved in this fire! I blamed him for me putting this hole in the wall and told him "Now I have to pay for the repair of a wall because of you!" I asked my son please never make me this mad again. Wish me luck with that request!

My most controversial topic on parenting and I get into the most trouble and almost fights is with my message to single mothers with sons. I often had to remind them that "He is not your man. He is your son. He is not the man of your house, he in the man in your house. You sleep with the man of the house, you are intimate with the man of the house and the man of the house has equal power as you. There is a big difference between "of" and "in". Do you want your son to be equal to you? He can help you make decisions or pay bills, however he is still in your home, still not on your level and still has no real power. The power he has is the power you give him. When you give up your power you give up your authority, your ability to lead and most of all your position of respect. He is never to have or be given power over you unless you can't grunt, blink, twitch or make some type of verbal or nonverbal communication to others to save you from this power driven savage. Teenage and adult sons are the hardest to get along with because they feel as they must set boundaries for you like they gonna get obeyed. However far you let them tell you what to do and how to do it is how far they are going to go. Mind you if you let them get too far, this route comes with different forms of disrespect and you will not like it! If you let the situation get out of your control, he will be a force to be reckoned with, such as the way he feels he has the right to treat you like he is your man. He will have comments and criticisms on the way you dress, where you go, who you talk to and how you spend your money just to touch on a few. You have to check them and keep checking them every time they get out of pocket and in your business. The kid must stay in his own lane and if he gets into your lane, crashes and messes up things then it is your own fault cause you allowed it. Maintain your position of authority at all times. He calls no shots and you do not let him think that he rules or controls you by speaking that he is the man of your house.

Chapter 3. My Daughter

The strongest one of the whole Team

Chapter 3. My daughter

In my team of survivors this was one helluva survivor. Even tho she kicked life's ass when the fight got unfair, I am going to take you on a journey down the darkest, heaviest hardest part of my life, losing my child. I suggest you grab some tissue your favorite source of recreation whether it be Kool-Aid, wine, coffee a stiff drink, a nice chair and get comfortable because I'm going to take you there. It was nothing more heartbreaking than losing a part of me. Watching a beautiful blue casket being lowered 6 feet into the ground with my heart in it and all I can do is stand there and cry with my soul breaking into a million and one pieces. My knees are barely holding me up, I wanted to let out an ear piercing scream of the pain I feel burning deep down in the pit of my stomach, It hurts so bad that I cannot even begin to describe or explain the emotions that are attacking me because I know that this was last time physically I am going to see my child except for in picture. I cannot touch her ever again! We cannot laugh together, we will not practice the latest dance moves. We will not grow together! We just will not be anything anymore. Could you imagine that? Experiencing that feeling in your wildest dreams or your scariest nightmares? Nope nothing can compare to that. Nothing!

I will start you on this journey of how our life was. It was full ride! She was my pride and joy. My little girl. I used to tell her it was us against the world. She was so smart and an interesting child. She made all the garbage i went through with the whole pregnancy thing worthwhile. Let's talk about the first major disaster she and I encountered. Our peace was interrupted by a terrible awful tragedy. At the age of six she got hit by a car as she was leaving choir rehearsal on a Thursday night while crossing the street. I was working evenings at the hospital and got a phone call from my dad who was at home and given the task of telling me this heartbreaking news. He was hysterical. He said that he had just gotten a call that my reason for living had gotten hit by a car and was on her way to the hospital where I worked. I immediately dropped the phone, turned around to my coworkers at the nurse's station. They say I mumbled something about emergency room, a car and my daughter and then I ran down four flights of stairs to the emergency room. One of nurses from the unit was on my heels to make sure I had someone with me. We were a close unit like that! I saw nothing and nobody as I was hauling ass getting to that ER! I was standing at the main emergency room desk when the status report came in on the loudspeaker from the ambulance. The paramedic said, "We have a six year old gir with severehead trauma with broken a right fibula and fibula. No pulse, unresponsive to painful stimuli! ETA 3 minutes. I lost my ability to think, to stand and that's when my my knees lost their ability to successfully do their job. To the floor I went. They immediately picked me up and put me on a stretcher. They were requesting to give me Valium 10 mgs IM until I told them "No, I am pregnant!" I was two months pregnant with my second child I was taking no drugs. I told them to let me get up off this bed. My legs were still unsteady so they put me in a wheelchair and wheeled mc out of the ER. They placed me in room with the rest of my family, church members and friends. I don't remember any other conversations and vague faces of the people there. I do remember the nurse coming and kneeling in front of me telling me that this was serious and I needed to name a neurosurgeon. The two hospital chaplains stood on each side of me with their hands on my shoulders. I knew they was praying. They finally got in touch with the neurosurgeon I requested and after two hours of waiting to see my baby and the uncertainty of what was going to happen, I finally got to see my baby, she was on a respirator with a large bandage on her head, she was not moving. I took her tiny hand and told her that I would be right there when she got back. All my coworkers and friends rallied around me and held me strong. Her surgery lasted eight hours and when the neurosurgeon came in to talk to us all he could say was that she made it through the surgery before he broke down crying like a baby. He said she died twice on the table but they were able to bring her back. He said all we could do is wait to see if the craniotomy he performed was a success. She was transferred to ICU where she was in a drug induced coma for days, I never left her side. My friends and coworkers finally got me to leave and rest reminding me that I was pregnant and I had to take care of me and the baby I was carrying. My live in boyfriend at the time was very supportive and loving. After all it was his baby I was carrying. His mother was always good to me and was by my side anytime she could. My family, my church family, my coworkers and my friends were also there for me. God guided me all the way! He kept me and never left me. Eventually she was transferred to the pediatric unit. They called her the "Miracle Baby", Because of what she endured and she made it through. She came out of the coma, but she was different. She talked differently and she acted differently. Nevertheless she was alive.

My most memorable moment in this whole situation was when she was transferred from ICU to the pediatric unit. She was still in a coma and they told me she would be a vegetable the rest of her life. She would be unable to do anything or care for herself. I would take my baby any way I could get her, atho I never accepted this diagnosis. This particular morning I was laying on a cot next to her hospital crib with my back to her. All of sudden I heard "Hello mother." I thought I was hearing things so I turned over and there was this bald headed little girl(they had to cut all her beautiful hair off) with this huge stapled surgical scar across her head, leaning over the bed smiling at me! She said it again," Hello mother." I could not say anything, I jumped up and ran down that hospital pediatric ward hall crying and screaming, saying she said "Hello mother! God is so good! God is real!" Everybody was crying tears of joy with me. It was a moment that i knew God heard me.

Her recovery and physical therapy went well. The accident left her with a scar and a crooked eye but she was alive and functioning. She was able to return to school, but she was different. She was determined and anything she wanted to do she did it. The head injury changed her. All the things they said she would and could not do she did it. Even with a thigh high cast she was turning cartwheels. Her mental status as she grew older was that her logic and reasoning was sometimes out the window. She struggled with this but somehow she managed. She would have blowups at times ad sometimes she would be passive. I learned the best of my ability to deal with a child with a right brain injury. She overcame so much and I was so proud of her.

She was told that she would never have children. Boy were they wrong.

She had two boys by the time she was 19 and at that age with 2 kids! She had a lot to handle. She loved her boys however her parenting skills had some gaps. I tried to help, however I was a young grandmother and I could have done more to help, but I needed help too. This girl was a piece of work

She grew into a talented young woman who could sing, and, draw and could handle her own. She was a true warrior and survivor. She loved the streets, she owned the streets and survived in them. There were times the streets were her friend but not mines. That is a whole nother something something. Raising a daughter is a whole novel by itself maybe two!

As she grew she worked toward bettering herself until one day at the age of 25 and pregnant again, she came into the house and said "Mama the doctor said I got Lupus and rheumatoid arthritis." "What was that you just said?" I asked her. She said "Lupus Mama, I got Lupus." I had heard about it the first time, but I had no idea what it was and what it would do to her.

So we began on this journey with her illness in 1998. She had so many episodes of hospitalizations as to where I had to learn about the disease and how to care for her. It wasn't something that I was really excited about as a matter of fact it was heartbreaking.. As the lupus progressed, oh yeah did I mention she was pregnant with grandson number 3, she got weaker.

So here she is with this diagnosis and pregnant. The combination of the two always had me worried about her. One day I just happened to go over to her house and it had stormed and everything so I went to see about her and the two grandchildren. She was laying in the bed sick for days and not telling no one or anyone. My motherly instincts kicked in, so what I did I took the two grandchildren to my mom and told my friend to take her to the hospital so by the time I got to the hospital she could have been registered and possibly waited on. By the time I got to the hospital they had admitted her to the Intensive Care Unit. She was that sick. She was there knocked out on strong drugs. Her skin was so dark and pasty looking she looked like she was dying. The doctor came out to me and said your baby is critical, it's a good thing you brought her in when you did. She will be here in the hospital for a while.

She came out of the Intensive Care Unit but she was blind due to the medicine that they gave her. She was on a lot of meds, so which one exactly that caused the reaction, we did not know. Her sight eventually came back to her after maybe a week or two but she was still so weak. She was transferred into a room on the gyne unit. One day after she got there the doctors came to me with a serious question, "Mother this is serious, you have to make a decision at this point. It's either the mother or the baby, which do you prefer?" What kind of sick joke is this? I mean really? I am not God! I looked at the doctor like he was crazy! He wanted me to play God. I could not do that, so I told him God told me I could have both of them and that's what I wanted. I stepped out on faith once again. Praise God they delivered the baby C-section and both baby and mom was fine. Recovery was going to take some time. In the process of her recovering she was given the warning that she should not have another baby because it would be bad for her body after the trauma she had just experience delivering grandson number 3. We got home she was doing okay, getting up and about after a while and then I know that she started getting sick and weak. We discovered that she was pregnant again. Baby number 4! She was sick but determined to have this baby despite what the doctors said.

She had just been thru a terrible ordeal and now she knows she has to go thru it again.

She stayed pretty healthy with this pregnancy until toward the end of her second trimester. She started swelling and her blood pressure was through the roof. She was a high risk pregnancy and was immediately hospitalized after a visit to her gynecologist. She remained hospitalized until the birth of grandson number 4. She remained in pretty good health just weak and tired at times and I helped her as much as I could with her babies. Her and the babies moved in with me and her brothers. I was so relieved that she was close so I could keep an eye on her health. One day I heard her scream "Gaddoggit!" and then I heard her banging on the floor over and over again. I ran downstairs as fast as I could to find her sitting on the couch with a shoe in her hand. Someone had sent her some clothes and as she pulled them out there was a brown spider in the midst and he somehow bit her on the front part of her leg. Needless to say she beat the insect to pieces with that shoe so I never got to see the insect in its whole form. As time went by the small insect bite began to drain, turn black and spread. She began to get weaker and weaker and thinner and thinner despite all the treatments she was going through. She tried to maintain taking care of her four boys but it wasn't easy. I didn't realize how sick my child was because she covered it up so well. I even went to the doctor with her to complain about her not getting better. I went into the room with her started complaining she looked at the doctor the doctor looked at her and needless to say I wound up in the waiting room with the children waiting her for her to complete her visit. Did she know she was dying then? Did she really know how sick she was and didn't want me to know? What was she hiding?

So as time went by she seems to be doing okay so I decided to relocate to Milwaukee Wisconsin. Her older brother had went off to college and her younger brother was in High School. So off he and I went.

I left Gary and everything in the house, she was living with me and she told me she could get the house together so I left her to take care of the house. Little did I know she couldn't do anything for herself, she put up a good façade and I fell for it. One night about 4 months later while I was in Milwaukee she called me and she didn't sound right, she was incoherent and disoriented. She kept talking about there was cereal on the floor. What she did say and I remember it so well was, "Momma I had to find the phone to talk to you, I crawled to find it." She sounded so strange and I kept yelling at her through the phone "baby please go to the doctor now! Go see about yourself please!" She said okay. The next call I got the next day was that my sister found her on the floor unable to respond. Here I am in Milwaukee with no money and the emergency room telling me that someone had to stay with her at all times. I was back where I was 21 years again! Living the same nightmare again! Lord help me! Please help me! She was not responsive and she cant take care of herself or answer any questions, but she was alive. My family immediately got together and got me to Gary Indiana. My cousin that I trusted through anything drove me there safely. I arrived at the hospital where she was. By the time I got there, she was in the Intensive Care Unit. They told me they were making plans to fly her out that night from Gary Methodist Hospital Northlake to Chicago because she needed more care and that the hospital that they were flying her to could give her what she needed.   At this time I agreed. The helicopter finally arrived, I was standing there just praying as they prepared her for the flight. We went outside to watch the chopper take off.

As the Chopper lifted off with my baby slowly into the air, my knees get weak my head got light and I just fell face-first into the shoulders of the person standing next to me. Thank God for family because I had cousins who were there with me at the hospital, they got me to the University of Illinois in Chicago. It took the helicopter 7 minutes to get her there and it took me 30 by car. I don't even remember who was driving.

Once I got there I remained at University of Illinois Chicago Hospital with her, by her side for 30 or so days. She underwent so many procedures and surgeries that I knew she was scared and so was I. My plans were to never leave her side until she left that hospital whichever way it went. Dead or alive I was going remain posted. I slept on floors, in chairs, in vacant patient rooms, the hospital staff tried to assist me in any way they could and I appreciated them for caring.

After they finished all the treatments and did what they could do for her they had the social worker come in. She was a nice lady and she had these papers with her, she said that my daughter was unable to care for herself and needed 24-hour care and they had assigned her to a Skilled Nursing Facility in Gary Indiana. All they needed was my signature. They gave me those papers early that morning and at 2pm that afternoon. I had still not signed them because it was hard for me not to care for my child at home. I wanted to. To just put her in a facility, a nursing home! That was hard, needless to say I never signed the papers but they transported her anyhow because they needed the bed in intensive care unit. She was so far away from home that hospital wasn't the proper place for her care and the social worker chased me around the hospital most of the day trying to get me to sign those papers. She saw the hurt in my eyes and the reluctance that I had a putting my baby in a nursing home, however she kept talking to me so I told her okay but I never signed the papers. When the ambulance got there loaded my baby on to the transport, I realized I did not have a ride. I was allowed to travel back with her but not back there with her. I was allowed to ride in the ambulance in the front. Even though she was going to a nursing home and not home, my heart was happy because she was alive. She was headed home and we had a long recovery process ahead of us. Just to see the sunshine and know that I had my daughter with me no matter what condition she was in because she was paralyzed from her neck down unable to speak but totally aware of her surroundings, I had her, I was taking her home. The reason I know she was aware is because I would ask a question and tell her to blink or either shake my hand squeeze my hand and most of all give me that Kool-Aid smile and she did. We arrived at the nursing home and they were very receptive and knowing that I was going around inspecting everything, every nook and cranny in her room they welcomed us. They knew I was looking to make sure that my baby girl will be in the best care. I stayed there for hours until they put me out. They told me "go home mother we got this" they said. One of my friends worked there so I knew that my daughter was in good hands. That was a little relaxing knowing that I could call someone and talk to them about my baby. She was 27 years old at the present time but she was in the shape of a newborn baby. That was okay with me she was alive

From the time my daughter got sick until I took responsibility, my mother and my sister were the caregiver of my grandsons. They were my rock I thank them from the bottom of my heart and love them for caring for my grandsons when me and their mother couldn't. Now I was ready to care for all my family, my daughter, sons and grandsons. I needed them.

I found all of us a house on the Eastside of Gary and I moved one son and my grandsons into the house where we could function as a family together. We were separated due to her illness and now we needed time to come together and love on each other, encourage each other and most of all, take care of the boys in their time of need because they were young boys and they were going through a lot being separated from their mother for 2 months. I'm at constant visits to the nursing home taking the boys, staying with her and just trying to help her with her rehabilitation but disaster struck, she got pneumonia! She was transported to a hospital where she stayed until they cleared up the pneumonia. They were not caring for her at the nursing home as I knew they should. One time I walked into her room and she had not been changed all day and on another time I walked into the nursing home and she had not been changed her bed was saturated with sweat and I was just not happy. I tried to be understanding and patient with this facility. Disaster struck again. She came up with pneumonia for the second time and as she was in the hospital as a patient, I contacted social services and told them that I was capable of taking care of my daughter at home. I would like for her to come home and have treatments or whatever she needed at home. They agreed and they began the process of getting ready to be cared for at home. That was in October she came home boys were more than happy to see and be around her. I was more than happy and her brother from college came home also. He decided that he was needed more at home then in school so she stayed home to help me with the boys. We all gave up a lot, but it was a decision that we agreed upon and wanted.

She came home. I called her my Million Dollar Baby because she had over a million dollars worth of equipment and that one house. I used to work at the hospital for 12 years so I knew pretty much what I was doing. I was now her caregiver. I had to do her daily dressing changes, get her in and out of bed, feed her, change her, bathe her and do whatever she needed to have done. She was paralyzed from her neck down and she was my baby. This way I could monitor her meds and her care. I was doing all I could, I was taking care of my baby. The nursing agency eventually sent me home services and the Nurses Aide would come in and make me leave home for 1 to 4 hours. She told me I needed to get out of there to get some air to clear my head and just keep on living. So I took her advice and maybe 2 to 3 days a week I would just go out and do something but all the time I was gone I felt like I should have been at home. I felt like I should have been there altho she was being cared for by the nurse and the nursing assistants and I needed to take this time for me. How could I when all that was on my mind was my daughter and her getting better.

The holiday seasons begin to roll around. Thanksgiving was the first holiday I was able to dress her, get her up, get her together and get her to the whole family visiting at Daddy and Mama's house. I was so happy and so was the family. Everybody was so glad to see her, she was smiling and kissing everybody. I was able to get her out of the wheelchair and sit on the couch next to my daddy and her aunt. I fed her and everybody loved on the fact that she was spending Thanksgiving with us and that was a real blessing.

Her 28th birthday rolls around we celebrated with cake and ice cream and guests. We sang happy birthday to her. We had cake and ice cream, people came over. We laughed, she flashed her Kool-aid smile frequently. She coming back this way!

Christmas rolled around I was able to get her up in the chair and enjoy Christmas with her sons opening their presents and everything. She stayed up for a while. We were a happy family. Even though she was sick she managed to smile and kiss me every day. It was her form of saying thank you Mama. she kissed me on Christmas. We had a great Christmas. She was even able to say Merry Christmas as I covered her tracheostomy up for her try to speak. We called one of my friends on the phone and she told her Merry Christmas and the next thing I know my friend was at my house bending on the bed where my daughter lay, smiling and crying. She was truly happy to hear my baby's voice and so were we. It had been a while.

New Years Day 2004 comes in with us all together at home enjoying each other and just being happy that another year together has come

January 5th 2004 is her third oldest son's 5th birthday rolls around we have lasagna, chocolate cake, ice cream and fun. She was able to at attend her baby's 5th birthday party and she ate some lasagna too. As I was feeding her she smiled with every bite. I looked at her smiled back and said, "girl you got a story to tell when you get better." She nodded her head

January 8th 2004 my baby girl seems a little bit happier, prospering smiling, just coming to life a little bit looking around I'm feeling good although that damn lupus had eaten her body up taking away all her weight just Destroyer I was putting morphine patches on there I mean it was awful anybody out there with lupus I feel for you because also paired with her lupus what's rheumatoid arthritis so she hurt constantly I did the best I could to keep her comfortable this particular evening it seem like the air went out of her hospital bed and the bed needed to be replaced so I had to take all the stuff that was hooked up to her bed off the bed and for the first time in her life she slept in the brand new bed that I had bought her since her illness. That particular night I slept in the bed with her and I know that she always told me whenever we slept in the bed together. "Don't touch me with your feet!" She hated for people's feet to touch her, so that's what I told her that night as we slept together. She just smiled. I hugged her and we slept peacefully side by side.

January 9, 2004, that day went well. We were happy with each other. Whatever happened in her teenage years and her younger years, we moved past that and all was forgotten and forgiven. We were in a mother daughter love affair. Our love was real.

She and I agreed upon is that she must get well and start being a mama to her wonderful sons because I knew that's what she wanted. They were her world. She was growing up with them. That is why I got all of us a house together, I knew being with her boys would help her recover. She loved the hell out of her boys. They were her reason for living and loving. If anything would help her heal, it was them. Love was strong in that household.

I got her up in the chair that day and my cousin came over and she talked to him. He was so happy to talk to her because he was always there for us and they always talked. The smile on his face said it all. He held me strong so many many times and i knew he was worried about us. He could relax a little. Later on that night I went to bingo with another cousin. My family was very supportive they wanted to keep me encouraged so they found activities for me. At about 9:20 p.m. my chest started hurting so bad my stomach started hurting, my left arm start hurting and I just laid across the Bingo table. I didn't know whether for them to call an ambulance or not. This happened for approximately maybe one or two minutes and then I was okay. I told my cousin I don't know what just happened but I thought I was having a heart attack, the pain was so crushing that it paralyzed me for a minute I just had to lay on the Bingo table. About 10:30 I get home, I walk in the room as I normally do and I said to her "Hey Mamacita!" She looked up at me and then dropped her head. I kept calling her name, no response I jumped on the bed and started shaking her! She wouldn't open her eyes! She wouldn't move! She wouldn't do anything! Talking about feeling like something was peeling your ribcage back and snatching your heart out with sharp nails. That was just a fraction of how I felt. At this time she was still warm and I just started screaming and shaking her, asking, no begging her to open her eyes to wake up! So I just grabbed her and held her so tight. As I was holding her I could feel the heat of her life leaving her body. Funny thing about that though, if you've ever watched a sci-fi movie, alien movie or anything like that, where you see where life is leaving one body going into another. I felt like her spirit was entering and combining with mine to give me strength to carry on with this journey I had before me. That's the feeling I had as I was holding her as she was transitioning. As I was holding her lifeless body i could feel her life! I believe it because Lord knows I don't know how I made it through some of the situations that I made it through. She blessed me with her spirit and strength. I believe truly in God and I know that he's capable of blessing us with anything. I ran downstairs to where my oldest son was and asked him "when was the last time you checked on his sister?" He said "Mama I just left from up there with her and I asked her did she need or want anything and she shook her head no." I looked at him with tears in my eyes and said "well son she's dead!" I did not know how else to tell him this heartbreaking news in the distraught state of mind I was in. I need to apologize to him for the harsh way I told him this life shattering news. Son I am sorry I wish i knew how to tell you better. I had no idea how to put one foot in front of the other correctly at that point. I knew i had to make moves tho.

I went back upstairs I had to start making calls and telling people what had happened. When we called 911 for an ambulance or whoever was supposed to come, they sent the police who came rushing into my house, lights, flashlights on going through the house. I had to stop the policeman and explain to him what happened and please do not wake this child who was sleeping in the room across from where his mother's body lie, to inform him that his mother is dead. That was the last thing I needed. He would have went crazy!!! They agreed and became a little more nicer and understanding to me. At this point people start arriving and my youngest son was coming home from basketball practice, got out of his friends car and saw the lights. They were used to the ambulance flashing lights, but I had to meet him outside and tell him the disturbing news. I grabbed him and held him so tight!. The scream of the pain from the bottom of his soul my son let out that night still rings with me today. My eldest son came and got his brother because I could not do anything after that. The sight of the two of them broken like that was more than I could bear standing on my two legs. I fell to the floor screaming and crying with my face in the carpet. I had my face buried in the carpet heartbroken with hurt, with no words to describe the pain, in that grief-stricken moment I was screaming. I could and did not want to feel what I am feeling because there are no words to describe what it feels like to lose a child. It is like hot boiling grease being poured directly in your heart. How am I supposed to feel? What am I supposed to feel? She was my adult child that I had grown up with. My daughter who was a mother. I felt I was no more, no emotions, no feeling, just numb. Dazed and numb, yep that was the combination of emotions.

About this point my husband at the time (we were not together), arrives and he goes in and looks at our daughter and just runs into the kitchen. , I happened to glance up and see him and he is standing there in the hallway with two big long sharp butcher knives, one in each hand, looking real cray cray! With tears in his eyes, he looked at me and asked me "Now can I cut this shit off my daughter, she don't need it no more!" In the midst of my tears I looked up at him standing there with tears in his eyes, hurt, with two big sharp knives in his trembling hands. It was hilarious and he was so serious! It was what I needed at that moment! I was laughing and crying at the same time. I told him no we have to wait for the coroner, then I would let him cut ALL the tubes off. When all the procedures were done, he cut all those tubes off of her, cussing each one out as he cut them off of his baby girl. Their daddy daughter relationship had grown strong thru the years. When they zipped her body up in that maroon bag, it was then and there he and I lost it. I remember very little from that point on. I want to say thank you to all the wonderful people who stood by me with me beside me and for me during this time I may or may not have said it I just want to put it out there publicly that you were so appreciated. I think you from the very bottom of my heart because I was walking around numb not thinking not knowing nothing and I had the best friends in the world to guide me around and family also this was a hard time for me I still have my moments but I keep getting stronger day by day.

The Wake

I must say I have some of the best people in the world in my circle because during this time they loved on me, they encouraged me and they kept me strong. They let me know it was okay to cry. Her wake was so crowded that people were standing outside and around and everywhere. She was well-known, well-liked by some and loved by many. My friends were my security that night. I have four to six friends that would let nobody close to me that they felt was up to no good or would say something that wouldn't sit well with me or upset me. Well this particular night I do not know what to say about them. My security fell apart. Here is what happened, we were all standing at the door of the funeral parlor inside, it was a cold Thursday night with some ice on the ground but none on the streets that we could see. Well one of my ex-boyfriend's decided he wanted to come to her wake, he came running through the door in a nice suit that was all dirty and soaking wet. They stepped in front of me like Wakanda warriors and stopped his pursuit to get to me. Standing in front of them, he told us I just wanted to come to me to tell her goodbye and somebody out of nowhere push me down in the snow in the middle of the street. He said "I didn't see anybody all I know is somebody pushed me in the nasty dirty snow!" Knowing his relationship with my daughter my friends and I begin to laugh hysterically I no longer had security, I had real friends who knew I needed a good laugh and I was. We had to go outside because we were laughing so hard and loud in a funeral parlor. Everybody knew that it was the spirit of my daughter that just pushed him down in the middle of the street and got him all dirty. If you knew her like we knew her you would understand why it was so funny, even in death she did not like him. She did that.

The Funeral

That dreadful arrived, January something, 2004. I cannot or I do not want to remember the exact date a piece of me was laid to rest with my daughter that day. I don't remember much about that day, just bits and pieces like how the funeral limo arrived how I freaked ran into the bathroom and locked the door to the point where I haD to be talked out by a very good friend of mine who I trusted all I can remember is running into the bathroom in my underwear and her talking to me through the bathroom door trying to convince me to come out which eventually I did. She even talk to me while I got dressed somehow I gathered enough strength to get me out the door to the awaiting limousine. All my fellas was in that limousine and all I knew was that I had to maintain in order for them to maintain. I just wanted to jump out the door of the limo, run, scream, stomp, kick or fight something and cry until I passed out. My thoughts were conveyed through my eyes and what they were saying loudly was, "Please don't make me go in that churchhouse, please don't make me do this! I can't do it! Help me somebody please!" Instead I put on my game face for my children and grandchildren. It was so hard but I did it, I had to for them.

We arrived at the church and family and friends with standing outside awaiting our arrival. The thing I remember that this was the church she loved, the pastor she loved, the man of God who had helped her turned her life around, and the sanctuary she loved attending had been renovated and the floors were so pretty and shiny. The reason I remember the floors so perfectly is because as I walked down the center, leading the procession of my family and friends I had the three year old on one side, the five year old and older soldiers flanking around me. Every step I took the casket seemed to get farther and farther away. I kept looking at the floor with every step asking myself am I going to be able to do this? Am I gonna make it? I looked around and at myself and I said you going to have do this. We finally made it up to the casket and I let every boy say his goodbyes and her brother as well. I remember my husband being right there with his family, as a matter of fact he chose his sons' wardrobe that day. He held us together whether he knew it or not. He was the man I needed and wanted to be there on the most horrible day of my life. I will forever love him for his love of his family first when they needed him even tho he was hurting too. The most traumatic thing I remember is the closing of her casket and begging with them my heart silently, please don't do that please don't do that because once it was closed she was no more physically which meant a part of me was no more physically. But they did and that is the part where I lost it totally! The rest of the day and for weeks I do not remember anything at all maybe fragments. I don't even remember how I got to the cemetery or was there a repast or what. I don't remember if I did this so I will say thank you any and everybody that offered me encouraging words a hug of smile or you did something for me or my family, I really appreciate you thank you

To my Warrior Princess you fought a hard long battle, your strength gave me strength to stand with you even in your toughest darkest hours. Every mother need to have a Warrior Princess, you were mines. You did not take a ounce of mess about your mother, brothers and sons when you were up and well, some sick days too. Yeah my Warrior Princess I know you looking down from heaven protecting us. This we know. We feel your presence. Damn you Lupus, rheumatoid arthritis, that brown recluse spider that bit her and that incompetent ass doctor that was supposed to be treating her. Because of you my heart is torn into so many pieces that I will never recover. For me to bury my adult daughter, their sister, their mother was one of most cruelest, devastating blows life could deliver and I had to stand strong to keep them strong. Talking about weathering a storm, this was a tsunami times 1000000000. We had to get thru this......together as a family and we did.

There is a lot of emotions that comes and goes with losing a child and all I can say is when that moment hits you at the grocery store, or at an event or maybe even by yourself all you can do is let the tears fall because as hard as you try to stop them, those tears are for a part of you that is no longer here, there or anywhere and they will not stop because you want them too. Yeah that's grief and you will forever have it and it's up to you how you deal with it.

Chapter 4. The Team

Now you see why my team is so strong.

Chapter 4.The Team

I gotta tell you about the fellas on my team of survivors. They are some interesting guys I have 2 sons and due to the death of my daughter I had 4 grandsons to raise too. I've been a mother since the age of 18 so child-rearing is not new to me. What is new to me is that the other day the youngest grandson who will turn 18 years old in May came home with his cap and gown talking about graduating and going to college! The reality of the end of my journey of parenting was hitting me hard in the face, this was it! I was not ready for this! I talked so much trash to them about what I was going to do when the last one graduated and here I am in my feelings. I could not let him see me cry, but I was thinking no more getting up in the mornings with the regular morning ritual of fussing, hollering, cussing and threatening them to make sure they got the hell out of my house on time to catch their bus, be at practice or whatever they was supposed to be doing. The tears fell.

No more checking out their different crazy male dress style for school. No more free breakfast and lunch, school mishaps, meetings with teachers and or school officials advocating on behalf of the education of my children. No more IEP meetings, SATS, parent advisory council meetings and that's what my heart fell. You see I had seven children in my house that attended public school and thru the years they kept me real busy with sports, activities and all kinds of scholastic activities before and after school.. Now there would be no more. The best part of this whole situation is that everybody graduated. Damn real. I have a perfect score. 7 students, 7 graduations. 7 high school diplomas. No fatalities because they did what was commanded and demanded of them. They knew the deal. They knew the consequences. They stepped up to the plate. They did their thang for education. They got that paper that made them good.

With this being said, I am going to give you a little insight on each of the fellas since I told you some of their accomplishments and endeavors. They are a real trip at times, but hey what can i say, they got it honestly. There are six of them, so i am discussing them in the order of hierarchy. I am not going to mention their names in ever in this book because I want to protect the guilty. As you read the remainder of this book you figure out who is who and which one of these creative characters did what. Why shouldn't I let you figure it out? I want you to enjoy them as much as I did and some of you reading this book was right there with me when some of these crazy or hilarious things happened. Right here, right now is where I present to you the fellas and their roles in my life.

The General.

I will start with The General because he is the oldest. He stepped in to help me with the boys after I had completed their formative years. As they got into their teens and taller the general told me he wanted to help me with the fellas, I agreed to the outreach.

 As the general, he is not open to reason at times, he rules with an iron hand and will have his army in step or back in step in no time flat. He is a no-nonsense type of guy and he hates liars. The General has a heart of gold and we'll make sure everything's taken care of and will not say a word, he is like Nike, "Just do it." When talking discipline, he believes very little once there is a discrepancy and gave the fellas very little opportunity to talk when he knew they were wrong, sometimes this is a good thing and sometimes it didn't go quite so well but after the general calmed down or the soldiers calmed down every thine would be discussed. The things he stressed was critical thinking, common sense and most of all thinking for yourself never being led by anyone other than him and myself and to always try to remain respectful, courteous and empathetic. The only thing that we had to really work with the General on as far as child-rearing is that when they had to answer to the general his patience was 1/8 of an inch from being gone. In order to be brought before the General, the situation is one I could not handle or deal with, he saw it for himself or the school called. When it got to this point, he was strict and unmoving in his role of disciplinarian. Talking about being a 6 foot 6 fixed foundation with no immediate reasoning, mentally and or physically, we had problems if you had to answer to him. Yeah that is a pretty good analogy of that one. However he sometimes he goes from 1 to 500 in .1 seconds and that's not good. His method was his method and I tried not to interfere because it was me who asked for his assistance in that particular situation. Talking about spontaneous Crazy Action Plans, the General's favorite form of discipline, because he doesn't too much believe in physical discipline, he believes and physical stamina endurance and the ability to think about what you have done wrong. His discipline of choice is the infamous wall sits, no harm no foul just pure strength and endurance. A few times the fellas swore up and down that they were crippled for life after having to serve their consequences with wall sits. They had to learn good negotiation skills in order to deal with this one. They hardly ever won trying to negotiate with him, but nevertheless they learned that skill and that's a good thing. Negotiation is a must in life.

Now there is a side of the general that is so wonderful that I have to tell you about it. This young man has such a great determination with skills and ability that make him extraordinary. He is 6 foot 6 in tall, a handsome chocolate drink that exhibits a personality that draws people. He is very close-knit with his friends and a kind of guy that you can depend on. He is stealth like in his movements and a great athlete. He is such a great athlete and he was selected to be the 2010 NCAA National All-American as he attended college. He was the strategy on the floor. When he played on the court, besides being a great leader, you can say he was also a great team player and that is what makes him as good as he is. At home he has led the fellas to amazing educational victories. The victories include completing school with good grades, being a good athlete, being a respectful person and going on to find their place in the world. Being built on a good foundation his friends love him and the people that are around him find him enjoyable because he is who he is all the time. One thing I can truly say he will be a great dad from watching and experiencing him the younger fellas, he is going to be a blessing as a father.

The most memorable experience I had with my General (Lord knows I have a lot of them!)that proved he was destined for greatness was when he was in the 10th grade he was a star basketball player he scored 28 points in his first game and he was outside playing basketball with his football with his cousins and his brother he went to catch the football and ran into a rose bush that pierce his eye. He had emergency surgery the next day where the doctor told him he would never play basketball again. I saw a tear roll from the good eye and he said to me as I sat in the waiting room so disappointed because I knew basketball was his life and at this point here is a 16 year old young man being told that was he loved he could no longer do. I remember this is as though it was yesterday, my son walked out into that waiting room touched me on my shoulder and said "Mama I'll be planning two weeks watch me!" I looked at him and total admiration and I believed him. He returned to school with a patch on his eye and his basketball coach was so hurt but the general kept telling everybody he was going to play again and he did! His shooting was a little off at first but he kept playing and progressing. He even earned himself a scholarship with one good eye! He is quite a guy and this people, is who leads our team. He knows as a leader that he is not always liked, agreed with and sometime can be an asshole in his decisions, however the case may be he is loved so very much and appreciated greatly in my life. He is my Strong Arm and every mother needs a strong arm.

The Ambassador

The team's ambassador is an exceptional one. He is the type of guy you would love to have on your team because he has traveled the world experienced a lot of different people, food, places and things. He is very articulate. He can speak well for and of the family.   He is our spokesperson. As well as the spokesperson, he is also our gatekeeper. He protects us at all cost under the direction of the general and sometimes under the direction of himself, he accepts very little supervision. He will not allow the family to be denigrated or talked negatively of he will also tell you off and think nothing of it. So what a better person to send out into the world as a representative of us? Sounds great doesn't it? Well when it is all said and done, he refers to himself as the Great. He holds that title near and dear to his heart and he does not take it loosely or lightly. The Ambassador is 6 ft 7 tall dark and handsome, very charming, charismatic and a great artist. He will steal your heart with his art. I always tell him "God kissed your hands!" when it comes to his artwork and paintings. He is a talented artist, singer dancer, business owner, father and athletes all rolled up into the gift of being left handed.

There is however another side of the Ambassador, the side that's the passionate leader in him. His leadership style delivery and his stature is sometimes considered intimidating. He's simply trying to get his point across and one thing for sure, you will remember him and his point, whether you agree with it or not, you will remember.

My memory of this one that will be forever be seared in my mind (Lord knows there a lot of them!) is when he was 2 years old. He was in a competition where he ran for the title of Mr. Gary Tiny Tot. This was a Citywide competition with the kids 2 to 3 years old that compete, showcase their talent and sell tickets to the show. The performance was at Indiana University Northwest Auditorium and the place was packed. We had rehearsed earlier that day and he was all ready for his performance which was "Man in the Mirror" by Michael Jackson. After we left rehearsal I made him take a nap. I woke him up and got him all nice and spiffy in his red and white. He had on white pants white shirt red bow tie red jacket and a pair of nice white patent leather shoes. On the way to the actual performance he seems a little aggravated. It seems he got aggravated because he had to take a nap and he didn't want to.   On the ride to the university where he was gonna shine bright like a diamond, I asked him he was ready. He said "No." I asked him, "Are you going to do it?" He said "No." Everybody in the car laughed and we all shrugged it off. Seems he was a tad bit pissed off because I made "the star" take a nap! We arrived at our destination, seeing that the people had met this young man at rehearsal they were in love with him already and eagerly awaiting his performance since he did not do it at rehearsal either, he was too busy clowning around. He was a little chocolate boy with big beautiful eyes, a big personality and he had captured the hearts of all the adults the kids, everybody. When it's his time for to perform, with the whole family in the audience and me backstage cheering him on making sure he was in place and everything. We were ready. I was a proud mom. Well when they called his name he ran out on stage, all cute and stuff, the music to the song was playing in the background and this wonderful darling grabbed the mic and do the worst imitation of Pee-wee Herman ever recorded in history. Pee Wee Herman was a fictional character that had issues back in the day, not particularly a role model either! The most disturbing part of this character was his shrill annoying voice with an even more disturbing laugh! Most of all he could not sing, dance or talk well plus he had a strange voice and funny clothes Needless to say the whole audience was laughing very very very hard while our family was sinking down in their seats from embarrassment and I was standing at the stage entrance with my mouth open so wide you could have driven a Mack truck through it. He not only ran out on the stage one time to do the most messed up imitation of Pee-wee Herman that came as a surprise to everyone, he ran out on the stage and did it again! Then he ran backstage smiling like he had conquered the world. Right then and there I knew my son had talent, he was not afraid to be his own person and when he said he wasn't going to do something he meant it. This is why he is my ambassador because he speaks and stands strongly, proudly and bravely. We just have to work on his passion sometimes and the aftermath of delivery, because it sometimes leaves destruction! He will go up against the best of the best representing or defending his family. I love and appreciate him greatly for this. Every momma needs a strong ambassador, one who will keep comments in perspective in a way you won't forget. Sometimes the Ambassador may need an ambassador!

The Thriver

      This grandson is the eldest and the one who did, will and can survive thru anything. We all admire his strength because he had been through a lot and stood strong. Even with this being said, he is the most logical of the bunch, he tries to find a common ground and compromise among us. He the one with the hard job! Still he tries. He is a great big brother and he tries to lead by example in all he does. He has work ethics that are superb. He is always on time and he shows up for work prepared for the job. He will get to work even if he has to walk or if he's sick. If you hire this one for a job you are guaranteed a thorough worker who is a self starter, knows the rules because he is a by the book kinda guy. He is quick in his wit and will chop you down to a size no longer than an ant's ankle and will do it very tactfully. He is however very frugal in his spending, he pays his bills faithfully and loans very little.. He is not into extravagance or flash, he is a down to earth, laid back young man. He is a man of his word and will hold you to yours. He will listen to your side of the debate, if he does or does not agree with you, his response is guaranteed to be memorable. His quick wit and sense of humor are qualities that makes this gentle giant more lovable. He keeps you laughing even in the toughest of the situations. He was built to be like that.

      My most memorable moment with this one is when we had a bat in the house and that bat seemed indestructible. There was a young lady who was our houseguest at the time who was helping us in this "fight the bat " moment and at this point. The bat was winning, we had no proper training, no in-service, no memo or proper bat fighting procedures taught to us or was this a given situation where we were supposed to know? Where was it written or even thought that we had to fight Batman, Dracula, Count Chocula or whoever the hell he was? We broke some furniture, got some cuts and bruises but we eventually weakened, not defeated, the bat. The bat flew into to the screen door and I slammed the door. Great move. Now we got to go outside, around the house and open the screen to let him out, my grandson nowhere in sight. The brave houseguest who was real thin and tall decided to be the hero and perform the feat and open the door. She realized that wasn't a good idea because when she opened the door the bat flew upward and did not clear her head and flew right into her hair! She running, screaming, hitting herself on the head, it was truly a sight. I was laughing so hard! (Yep I am that kinda friend) The bat eventually got untangled from her hair flew away. Still no grandson. We finally make it to the front porch and there was my grandson sitting on there with this look on his face. We made it through the bat fight to where he was and he simply looked at us with a straight face and said, " I was sitting at the desk and a bat flew past me. I got outta there. I woulda helped you all if I was just a little more brave. That bat looked big!" We all just broke into hysterical laughter. How could I be mad at such honesty? He had made up in his mind he was not having it. He knew he was scared and was not going to force himself to play the hero. The bat won with him too.

The Brain.

Grandson number 2 is the one that knows all, sees all and has done it all if you mention a conversation or topic that he is familiar with. He is my go-to guy when I need information or research and he will research it until he's familiar with it and can verbalize it in the manner and what you can understand, after all he was reading on the 7th grade level in the third grade! So I know that when he says he's going to look up something and get back to me, it is going to be correct. He might have a long story with it but he's going to bring it and bring it well.

This fella is unique for his age. Let's just say you better bring your A-game when having A conversation with him. He has a strong willed personality and he thinks he is right about everything and unless you have concrete evidence to prove him wrong, he will remain right and let you know about it.   That's not a bad thing. Okay sometimes maybe it is not so great to have a strong willed know-it-all and sometimes it's great because you realize that this child knows exactly where he's headed, will not be side tracked and knows exactly what it takes to make it in life successfully.

Here's one where I had to bring my A game successfully. He was always breaking his glasses a day to a week after he got them. So once again I got him a new pair glasses. He liked them we like them and they look really nice on him. He went to school the next day with his new glasses on I was waiting on him to come home and see how his day went. 5:30pm rolls around he was not there. 6:30pm rolled round and he was still not there. I began to worry because this one usually comes straight home from school. A little bit after dark he comes in the door and I'm relieved. My best friend was there with me waiting for him to get home. So I asked him where was he.   Here's the story. He said he was jumped by two people and one guy on a bike and they broke his glasses. He just got those glasses! Something is not quite right with this story. Here's where my detective skills came in, he wore white...all white that day,   including sparkling white gym shoes to school. He comes in the house with all white including the gym shoes after a fight, tells me that they throw him down and kick him in the back and stomp all over them and break his glasses. What he did not realize is that I evaluated his clothing situation as soon as he came in the door. Now he tells me he's been jumped on and stomped on and kicked and he was wearing all white, which at the point he came into the door was still all white. I asked him what kind of guys was he fighting that they left his clothes clean? There were no footprints on him, his pants was still creased, with no smudges but he was in the fight where he was kicked and thrown down on the ground. I asked him how where they careful that they didn't get your clothes dirty? My best friend who was there looked at me like I was crazy because I was asking him these strange questions, but these are questions that I needed to ask after he had been in a fight and he had on all white. Please I need to know what precautions they took to keep you clean or what causes you took to stay clean after a fight. My inquiring mind needed to know just how this went down. Needless to say the only thing that was damaged was his glasses which were broken in half. He stuck to that cock and bull story and I have nothing else to go on, so as it stands right now he was beat up by three guys, two walking and dude on the bike that broke his glasses and left his white clothes nice, clean and bright. That is one for the books. You figure that one out. I did not.

The Gladiator

This is the first miracle of the bunch. This one is called the Gladiator for a reason and that is he is one to take on anybody at any time when he feels he is right. Sometimes this is good and sometimes not so good. He will fight, be angry and don't see anything wrong with his actions if he believes he's right. Whether he right or not is he believes he right and he is going to stand up and go toe-to-toe with you no matter what the consequences. If he believes he's right you have to go through a systematic way of proving to him that he is not correct. You have to go step-by-step and make sure that he is understanding what you are explaining to him or the whole thing is not valid. He has things on a set pattern and in his mind and this is how it's supposed to go and if one thing is out of place he is totally discombobulated and ready for action whatever it is. He is a sweetheart as long as things are in place and functioning as he planned them, he is in a comfortable spot but if it's out of pocket or out of sync, he's out of pocket and out of sync. When he gets likes this you have a mental or even a physical battle with this gladiator.

This one is a musical prodigy, he taught himself how to play the piano and if he hears a beat or a melody, he can play it after a while without ever having read the music. As a matter of fact he can't even read music! But now he is able to read it a little after watching piano videos. I must say this is quite impressive because we never knew he could do any of that because he's sort of a loner and stays in his room. Then one day we heard this beautiful music coming from his room. He was playing it! Wow!

He had real bad acne all through school and through all of the bullying and cruel remarks about his face, he stayed the course. He did not know it but there were times I cried for him because of the cruelty of people with looks and remarks. He took some tough blows as a kid with some of them coming from adults! Those adults did not know know how close they were to putting their ass where their mouth was! This grandmomma bear was ready to tear them to pieces! Say it again! Better yet let me hear you say anything about his face! We will be having a noncommunicable relationship with you not liking my actions. My gladiator needed to know another gladiator had his back!

He is also so lovable so compassionate and has a quick wit and a crazy sense of humor. He's an all-around good kid who requires a little special extra attention and love. All in all he's a great young man with a whole lot of talent and heart.

The story I want to share with you is about his early childhood. He was born prematurely and he had some struggles. His mom had struggles too because this is the baby that she pregnant with when I discovered she was really sick and diagnosed with the illness of Lupus. She was in her second trimester. She managed to bring this baby into this world with him having some health complications. So he grew up in the house as a little infant that we had to be careful with. We were his caregivers and we did everything for him because we thought he could not hear or talk for two years almost 3 years. In this time span he did not talk, so being a grandma that I am I started doing my little self test on him to see if he could hear. I remember one day clearly whispering "I have a sucker for you in my purse" and he was walking halfway across the room, he stopped turned around and waited for me to get that sucker out of my purse. I knew it! He understood a lot of things we said to him, he just didn't respond. I got a strong willed one on my hands! On this particular day he had gotten into some mischief and I was going to spank his hand. His uncles and brothers was standing around as I told him to "stick out your hand!" The fellas were protesting and almost crying to me that he did not understand because he could not hear. I told them yes he did understand and that he could hear. They were almost in tears thinking that I was being mean to this poor baby that was a victim of his circumstances. Then all of sudden when he slowly stuck out that hand to me in front of them! The look on their faces was one for the books, because for two almost three years he had them convinced that he could not hear or talk. Things changed around the household after that incident because the fellas tightened up their uncle game with   What it made me realize that he is quite a character and he will do only what he wants when he wants how he wants. But one thing he definitely knows, no matter what the weather, is that I'm in charge.

The Completion

As I go into the very last fella, he told me he wanted to be described in this book as "The Completion." He said that he was the finish to the end of the finished products. He said that he had so many accolades that I could not address him properly in just one term, so he gave me the term completion. Hell I shoulda let him write his own stuff since he so smart and got so much to say. Naw its my book, I am going to do it.

As we venture on into the story about the very last one, I love to talk about this fella, he's smart, he's handsome he's creative, he's entertaining and most of all he had the resilience and the stamina to endure a lot as a young man. He has proven over himself and over again. He's the second miracle out of the bunch, because during her pregnancy she stayed in the hospital with him five months with her blood pressure up and her knees and ankles swollen and on strict bed rest. She was a high risk pregnancy. She fought to keep and have this one and she did. He was born on time and was a healthy baby. His mom was in fair health even after the ordeal she had just experienced. After 5 months I finally drove mom and her cute little baby boy home.

As he was growing up I realized this one has the personality to attract all types of people. He can enter a room knowing no one and before he leaves a lot of people in that room know him. He is very affectionate and likes hugs. He has a charming smile that goes along with his personality. He sees the good in everybody and tries to remain positive by putting his faith, time and belief in God. A young man like him is a blessing. He just needs to remember his dirty plates and mess goes with him.

I have a story that I really like to share about this young man and it's about when he was younger that's about three or four. He loves the idea of being nice neat and clean so much that he would change his clothes five and six times a day. I mean he be going upstairs in one outfit and come downstairs in another. We found this amusing because we had no idea what he would come downstairs in the next time he came down. I mean he will come downstairs fully dressed in a suit sometimes he'd come downstairs in a jogging suit. Sometimes he would come downstairs in shorts. Whatever he decided to put on they matched at times sometimes they didn't, he did not care. He would just change his clothes like that in a snap! I often asked him " Who does your laundry? Do you have a maid? Do you have a wardrobe assistant up there or something?" I needs to know!

What I remember about this particular day because I had met a new friend in the city that I we relocated to. She was coming over my house for the first time to visit. I told the children that she was coming over and to be on their best behavior because she was an attorney. I wanted them to be good. Well this particular fella went upstairs after our "talk" and just as she was coming through the door he was coming down the stairs from the very top. He was donning a silk smoking jacket with an ascot. She looked at him and then looked at me and this is another time in my life I was speechless. Blindsided again! When he got down to the bottom of the stairs, he greeted her with a "How do you do Madamme?" with a French accent! Now that's a rich personality. When I told him to be on his best behavior I guess that was it. She was impressed and we laugh about it. A little French black boy!

There are so many episodes that I've had with these fellas that I would have to write at least 300 more books because they have put me through some situations. I have experienced some crazy hilarious and crazy serious situations and I know there's still more to come. I got a part of their mother with each one. Ask me if I would do it all over again. First of all I would tell you that I would not wish raising six males from boyhood to manhood as a single black mom/ grandmother on my worst enemy. You got to be prepared for a world that you can't even begin to imagine existed. But if you keep consistency and boundaries as your weapons of choice, you may be able to escape with a reasonable portion of sanity. You will be battered, bruised, torn up mentally and emotionally. Financially you are a wreck, but just know you will have the victory once they take ALL of their things and leave your house to find their successful destiny so they won't have to come back. You smile, help him pack and even try to cry, but deep down in your heart and mind you singing, breakdancing, getting your "he gone" party plans together. You learn so many faces as a parent to convince them that you are serious and right at that very moment when he is leaving you exercise that skill. My favorite is the poker face. Works every time. Yeah parenting does that to you. It makes you do crazy, silly, crooked stuff.

Chapter 5. Discipline

Getting them to see things MY way!

Chapter 5. Discipline

Being a parent has no job description, no paid hours and services on demand whether we want to or not with no invoices. When you have children you have to go above and beyond the any means necessary. What I mean by that is that you have to push yourself and put yourself in positions that are sometimes uncomfortable and not rewarding but remember you made the choice to be a parent, so all the characteristics, favorable or unfavorable, you got to flow with it, around it, into it and about it. Whatever "It" is, "It" is all you. Parenting "It" is not a piece of cake, however it is a slice of the pie. Your piece is your piece. You get what you get. The slice size is up to you.

Another important thing to mention is when you allow your kids to spend time at other people's place of residence, know what kinda lifestyle is going on in that house. As a parent you don't let nobody else put thoughts or actions that differ from your life teachings into your kid's head. If you don't teach them yourself other people will put into your child's head their version of what they want them to know and it will be their way, right or wrong. If you not teaching your kid about life, don't get mad if they learn from somebody else. It may be not the way you want him to learn, but hey, you shoulda did it yourself and you would have known how he knew, what he knew, when he knew it and who taught him.

I used to wonder why a certain family member would not send his children to everybody's house. Now I understand the reason why. Everybody is not you. Everybody is not going to treat your child the way you treat them. So you must be an active parent(s) and have and be a part no matter who's around or who's doing anything for your child as long as it is legal. It is your child! Know what people are teaching your baby. Also as the active parent(s) you have to establish the foundation with respect, discipline and love and all that goes with it. Parents sometimes we fall short and the child gets the best of us, but if we stray away and give up, the child wins. You find yourself pinned on the mat by somebody you been taking care of since day one, longer than that if you count the pregnancy. This is the last thing you want. Your kid in charge of your household. He the parent, you the kid. He telling you what where and how to do things. That really doesn't work out well for both parties involved. Just ain't right, my kid yelling and cursing at me telling me what to do. Keep your power, cut that shit off when it starts! All they need is one dance to your music. Just one dance and make it so they never want to hear that music again.

Another important thing I want to reinforce that I learned in my parenthood journey is that I had to be active and engaged in all areas of their life. Yeah sometimes they get mad because they think I was trying to get into their business. I was. I used to tell them, "Guess what? As long as you under my roof you ain't got no business! Your business is my business! Any question?" I had to be concerned and care about even the smallest things they get involved in and I had to be the head decision-maker and advocate for my child. Don't let nobody else do it for you. You do it. This I learned the hard way for free.

With all that being said let's talk about discipline and how I effectively disciplined my boys. I ain't saying my way is the way to go because nothing really works all the time. It is trial and error and some "oops" moments. You see because with this thing called parenting there is no guarantee, no warranty, no money back and you stuck with what you got. No returns to manufacturer. I got boys and boys are somehow different to discipline. They can step up and withstand some of the hardest blows including but not limited fists belts, ironing cords, switches, extension cords Hot Wheel tracks. You name it I have maybe tried it, some with good results some with not good results for me. So there were times, a lotta times had to put on my thinking cap. They gotta understand I mean business right here and right now. Time to take them to "I am the Parent Academy". What can I do that is nonviolent and thought provoking? Being the creative creature that I am, I searched my Crazy Action Plans playbook to find some solutions. What I found was the most effective for my boys at that time was to hit them where it really hurts. One day while they were at school after they had got on my last nerves and then some, I decided it's time for Mom to show them how it's done. I confiscated their cords, their adapters, batteries and power surge strips. Everything and anything pertaining to making electronic equipment work I locked them up and put them in a toolbox in my trunk. Next Step was to prepare them to have an effective way of showing me that they had completed their chores. I prepared the sign in sheet, a check off list and extra credit list as effective way of getting their attention. I'm going to do one of the ways that a young woman who was staying with me told me this was her father's way of discipline. So I kind of revised it to suit my method. What they had to do was sign in, select a chore, check it off and sign out with the time they completed it. One of their brothers or nephews would go behind them and make sure it was done and initial it then in turn to show the person completed it. They would get one to two hours of entertainment time which means they could get an electronic of their choice and enjoy it for that time. They had to sign out the piece of technology and sign back in when they completed with it. It worked effectively for a while and I was pretty happy with it but the paperwork turned out to be a little bit much for me because I too had to check everything behind everybody. I was on punishment along with these fellas. I ain't like it but it worked.

Another form of punishment that didn't require me to be present unless I voluntarily wanted to be is that I waited to at night when they got their school clothes together, cleaned up their gym shoes, posed a couple of times in the mirror and after trying them on make sure they look cool for school he go to bed. I would take their shoe strings, socks or one sock or maybe even the entire outfit confiscate it and or hide it The next morning I would watch them search high and low for their stuff and when they asked me I gave them a simple "I don't know why you asking me about something that is yours, you should have taken care of your stuff." I would watch them frantically put together a whole new outfit of some sort trying to replace the piece or pieces that was missing while I stay my room with the door shut laughing my ass off. I bet they will put your stuff where you can find them and not leave it all over the house!

Another form of discipline that I chose to use was with the school check out. When the school called me I would go and check my child out for approximately 15 and 30 minutes and have a nice conference with them whether it be in the school bathroom, or my sister who lived close bathroom or even a close friend's bathroom maybe even the park, but we were going to confer and after the conference we left the place with a great understanding. I explain to my child that my office hours start immediately when they leave for school and in when they arrived home I asked my child why was he messing with my time?

How many times did I have to tell them, "Do not physically fight your brothers! I don't care what you gotta do ?" Too many.

This brings me to conflict resolution. Conflict resolution was another form of discipline I taught them. It is how to get along with each other resolving issues. Don't get me wrong, we had no fights that I know of. There might have been wrestling matches but no fist fights that I know of. There have been sometimes when I came home and found things broken or misplaced or the boys resting early in the day and it all seems suspect, but they reassured me that everything was okay convincing me that they didn't have any kind of discrepancies amongst each other or anything like that. They said it was just that kind of day or they tripped over the piece of furniture or there were just tired. Then later on in life they decide to tell me what happened that day or confirm my suspicions that was in the back of my mind. I knew something happened between these two. They too nice to each other right now. Another thing I had to teach them about conflict resolution is forgiveness.. I had to subliminally or just nudge it in for them to forgive your brother or speak to your brother. Talk to your brother, talk to your uncle and i would give them one of my famous stories for them to get the message. There had to be a story behind it or some type of motivating force because men are so stubborn even when they're wrong and they know they wrong! Grandson number 7 told me it was "prideful instead of stubborn, but prideful is such a manly word because men are full of pride." I guess he called it right because I have always had to ease them into the situations with my motherly, grandmotherly charm and my winning personality, my love for them, a few threats with bodily harm and somehow I always seem to have gotten the situation resolved.

Now you know I got to talk about self- discipline. We as moms of young black sons (some older ones too!) really have to do is hold ourselves accountable too. We have to hold ourselves to a certain standard. When our kids get in trouble, succeed, advance or whatever the situation may be directly or indirectly we have accountability for them. We are responsible for them. How they act, what they say, what they do. So therefore there must be acknowledgement and if the situation warrants it, consequences for their actions. Here is where the complicated part comes in where self-discipline is a must, when dishing out consequences you must realize you too have to suffer same consequences to maintain consistency and for it to work. I learned you got to be in the mix for you to receive maximum satisfaction for this session of act right. In other words you got to be there! Your plans for the kid is your plans for you! He on punishment you on punishment! Consistency is the key. Raising kids is a mental war too. Even in the toughest battle just remember the main objective is this kid will never win. It will make a better person out of him. Better not perfect. They only little replicas of you in some shape, form or fashion.. How would you battle you?

Another hard part about being a single mom is even when you have support of your friends and family, you have to realize that you have a part in certain situations and sometimes the truth is not pretty or favorable and they will tell you. Admit it before they do! Just because you're the parents does not make you always right. (But if you can get away with it COOL!) You are capable of making mistakes and bad decisions, accept the fact that you are not always correct!

Then you have situations when one of the team decide he want to step out of the box and talk to you in a mannerism that's unbecoming of your child and you have no one to turn to you just feel like you been stripped of all emotion, all feelings you have you when your own child steps across that line! What I mean is being disrespectful to a point where you don't know how to handle the situation. you don't know what you're going to do, if it's

68

going to be legal or illegal. All you know is that you are going to do something to that child you for those actions!

After your initial shock of the kid's action and possibly your reaction, you have to take time to communicate and make sure the that the boundaries that were crossed are known and understood and never crossed again.

Crazy Action Plans

Crazy action plan. What is a crazy action plan? Well to sum it all up with my definition, it is a situation in a situation that requires a situation. It may be mental or physical. It may be drastic it may be dramatic it may be creative, it may be whatever you need it to be at that moment, it must be designed to get an immediate response. Crazy plans also include rules. The rules are from 1 to Infinity with the number one rule being the finite rule. Rule #1 is YOU WILL NEVER WIN! I will and may number the rules from 1 to whatever but it all comes back to Rule Number 1. I AM AND WILL FOREVER BE THE WINNER! YOU WILL NEVER WIN! This means even if I have to step back and regroup, I am going to emerge the winner.

Chapter 6. They Think "She Crazy!"

Ain't nothing wrong with a little crazy as needed.

Chapter 6. They Think "She Crazy!"

"She crazy!" How many times did I hear my boys say that to each other or other people? Perhaps at times I might have been a little unorthodox or off the hinge or chain or just plain crazy. I wonder if they would say those things to describe my actions? They did shit that made me unhinged! They made me act crazy! I only acted a little crazy anyway.

Let's talk about incident with one of the fellas when he was angry, I mean angry about us not having much so he decided to have a temper tantrum. I don't do temper tantrums well. He went in the kitchen of and proceeded to knock stuff off the table saying "We don't need any of this stuff!" I had just went to a food pantry and when he headed to the kitchen of course I followed him. He did not like the idea of his family having to go to a food pantry. Looking at him in amazement as he messing up my kitchen and talking crazy, so instead of adding fuel to his fire with my anger, I decided to take an alternate route. Instead as he was knocking stuff off the table and kicking stuff around, I decided to get in on the action and snatch the curtains down saying, I don't like these ugly ass curtains no way!" I then threw the kitchen table chairs out of the open back door, "they don't" match!" I started tossing canned goods to the floor, i looked at him and I told him "I don't like none of this here stuff either anyway! It is a bunch of shit!" He stopped what he was doing and looked at me as if he had seen the ghost. I guess he didn't believe me when I told him I had the number one crazy gene because I created and birthed him. I also told him my genes carried over to him and if he wanted to continue we could. I got the highest crazy trait. We could tear this whole damn house down! We would see who could out crazy who! I am game! Needless he stopped and was upset by my actions. I am happy to say another outburst like that didn't happen again. No more knocking my stuff around whether you like it or not. Keep walking and keep your thoughts and incorrect actions to yourself. This is something i had to reinforce from time to time with Crazy Action Plans in full effect.

The next time I had to exert my craziness is where one of the fellas was younger and he kept tearing up all my stuff. I mean everything I had he would tear up. I soon get tired of telling him to stop, so I decided to put a Crazy Action Plan in play. He likes to collect wrestlers, you know the miniature wrestlers. The little wrestler collector. I mean he had a collection of them and one day I asked him which of these do you like the best and he showed and gave it to me. Wrong choice Joyce! So I proceeded to go in the utility room after I had gotten the wrestler from him, put on my coat and told him to put on his coat. We went outside, it was a cold snowy day gloomy and everything. The snow was kinda high and here we are standing outside at the door with his favorite wrestler in my hand. I looked at him, he looked at me. The next move of crazy Action Plan # 623 was to sling that wrestler as far as I could across the yard in the snow with him watching me. The look on his face was priceless and worth everything of mine he touched and destroyed. Go tear the snow up and get yo shit! See how you like that! At this point he KNEW I was touched in the head. Yeah it was a little harsh but with these fellas you cannot show any regret any remorse or any type of weakness or they got you. Get them in a position where they understand your pain. Then go somewhere and laugh at yourself by yourself or with friends later.

The best one yet is when one of the fellas was acting up in school. They knew better! The school called me but they weren't aware of who I was yet. I was new in Omaha so they were not aware of Miss Willie, so when I arrived at the school in a big nappy wig, my long housecoat which was multicolored, a short jacket, big hoop earrings, a pair of pants that didn't match nothing I had on and some tattered too big turned up over gym shoes. Yep that was my wardrobe for this event. Everybody looked at me in amazement when I arrived at the school. I told them that they had called me and I was coming there to see about one of my prized possessions. Looking real amused,they gave me the pass his classroom. I went and I stood outside the door and beckoned for the teacher to come. She came to the door to talk to me trying to keep a straight face. I was looking real unfamiliar and fashionably uncoordinated. The stage is now set. I asked her send my grandson outside to me because I needed to talk to him. She did gladly and with a smile. The look on his face when he came to the door and saw me and what was wearing was worth all the money everybody reading this book put together! I got the desired effect I wanted! The look of total shock and embarrassment. Yeah! I was not finished yet, it was coming to be the changing of classes and we were in the hall when the bell rang. He tried to duck and die to get away from me but my crazy plan number 18 was in full effect! I was able to catch up with him and tell him loudly in the hallway how much I loved him! I followed him to his next class waiting for everybody to look at me and go in. I followed him and sat next to him and once again I told him how much I loved him loudly. I followed him to a couple more of his classes during the day because I didn't have anything else to do that day so I had plenty of time on my hands to harass him like he harassed the school. How could he be so lucky!? He acted up on one of my far and few free days so I found and put on my clown suit just for him! He did not like that! I did not care, I did not like his behavior! I told him that he would rather deal with his behavior with the school than the school call me and I have to deal with it. I told him my "kid free" hours were Monday-Friday from 7:30am-3:30 pm. I won't call him and don't call or have anybody call me for him unless it is crucial. Maybe he should have asked me what makes things crucial. This was one time his question asking ass did not ask the right question. This was not a crucial situation. This cost him. He had to pay. He learned that day just how "crazy" I was when it came to his education. Since I was in the loving spirit, his favorite cousin also attended the same school at the same time so I decided to do a drop in visit on this 7th grade young man too. He was and wasn't glad to see me because the look on his face was worth more than that of my fella's. I know he want to put his hoodie on and run as far away from me as he could. Not that day! I even made them take pictures with me! Talking about having a fun day, I had one that day! The school, the principal, and the security, everybody got to meet Miss Willie Williams that day and from that day on they knew I was serious about education in my house.

I think this will be the last one I talk about because this is I think my most prized crazy "she crazy" moment that i am going to share, however I got a million of em! This time one of the fellas decided to mouth off at me he was about 17. His mouth was real slick. I wasn't having that garbage! You never will out talk me or talk to me like I got a tail! I dunno if I said that out loud or I thought it, anyhow I got the broom because he was so tall because I knew one of my punches would not even phase him. I proceeded to swing at him with the broom handle, he grabbed the handle with both his hands and try to retrieve it from me and in the process he gave me a shove. I was standing in front of a couch and the shove caused me to fall over the back of the couch. I was in total disbelief that he had done that! I think I was in shock that I tumbled over the back of the couch.   He ran upstairs to his uncle's room for cover, and somehow his uncle convinced me that I was not in the right frame of mind to discipline the boy.   Of course he was correct so I chilled.   In the process I had chill time and out of my chilling I came up with Crazy Action Plan number 1! When I put Crazy Action Plan number 1 into play there's no hope for that fella. Crazy Action Plan number one requires careful planning and thought.   It is to leave a message that is like when he 40 he still will be sweating when he wake up realizing that I am crazy. So on with the story, I could not retaliate in the fashion that I really wanted to, so all day I terrorized him. Because he was so scared of what I was going to do to him that he went in his room and did not come out all day. Of course I followed. If he went to the bathroom I was posted up just looking at him when he came out. I would go to his bedroom door and knock sometimes softly sometimes loudly and I would repeat this sentence to him "I am going to get you. I don't know where and you don't know when, it maybe today and maybe tomorrow and maybe next month and maybe next week or maybe an hour from now but I am going to get you!" and then I would kick the door. It soon got to be dark, i am still mad and I went to bed fully dressed in black. I woke up in full vengeance mode. I turned off the lights in the house at 2:31 a.m. I looked at the clock so I know. I began phase one of my crazy action plan. The poor scared young man slept on the couch in the open in the living room for fear of being in a locked enclosed area with a crazy mad momma roaming the house. So with all the lights off in the house I carefully crawled on all fours, stealth like over to the couch where he was sleeping. I checked to see if he was sleep. Yeah he was sleep! You big dummy! I checked again to make sure he wasn't playing sleep, so at that point I lunged into action! I put him in a Nelson, whether it was a full nelson or half Nelson wherever it was, he woke up really in shock! I told him "Don't you ever in this lifetime as long as you are black and in America do anything that might cause me any type of bodily harm or injury! Don't even let me think you wanna get physical with me!

Did i not tell you I was going to get you?" The fear in his eyes was enough to let me know i got his attention and we understand each other. Mission successful.

I could go on and on because out with six boys and one daughter I got a lot of "she crazy" moments. When I have to reach into my Crazy Action Plan book and come up with a remedy for the solution, my main objective in parenting is that I always win. I stress to my children that I always win. I also stress to them that I am the top Warrior and they are unworthy opponents because they lack that age, expertise and ability to win a battle against me because I choose the battle and the battleground and it will always be to my advantage.

Chapter 7. What Just Happened?

Really??!!

I cannot even make this shyt up!

Chapter 7. What just happened?

A lot of crazy things that happened in my life that I need to share. Trust me they were crazy and I would like for somebody else to take this journey with me. I'll start with I learned a I lessoned from being the great sociologist that I am. A real great way of saying I was being inquisitive. Nosey in other words. I was at Methodist Hospital in Gary IN working in housekeeping. That's a *whole nother* story I will discuss maybe in another book. I was in my early trimester of my third pregnancy but I was having complications so I had to have a light job. So they decided my job would be cleaning elevators and the ashtrays adjacent to the elevator. This particular evening the hospital lobby was full so I had myself a ball walking around talking and being of good cheer as I normally do. I was pushing my little cart around looking like I was working, but in reality I wasn't actually doing anything but talking. It was close to the end of visiting hours so I resume my job and I took the elevator all the way down to the low lower level to work my way up. It was pretty dark as I got down there and if anybody know this sistuh I am pretty scared of anything darker than me. As the elevator doors open I am peeking slowly around the doors to see if there is anybody down there other than me. You know the scared way of looking at something slowly. Yep and there was a reason my spider senses kicked it, it seems there was a chair directly across from the elevator door with a white plastic grocery bag in it. "What's up with this plastic bag laying In this chair?" I thought to myself. "This is strange and you gonna just leave it alone" I said to myself. As you can see I talk to myself a lot. This time I was not listening to me and curiosity got the best of me. I walked over to the chair I looked at the bag and thought to myself once again, "what if this is a bomb?" Another thought came flying out of this amazing atmosphere into my head, "what is this is a bag of money?" Now I am truly really curious! Either way I decided to investigate, I touched the top of the bag, I touched something that was round and hard! What the hell is this? I backed up slowly and proceeded to go up the stairs to the lobby to where I knew security was. I am such a joker that people sometimes don't take me serious but this is that one time I needed them to take me serious The lobby was full of people and I did not want to alarm anybody but I was scared and I knew my scared ass needed to remain calm, so I walked up to the security guard and said to him softly, "there is a bag of suspicious origin in the basement in a chair in front of the elevator." I need you to come with me please. I was so cool that my name should have been Chilly Willie! He looked at me and saw that I was not smiling or cracking anything that resembled a smile. He must have seen it in my face that there was something really going on. He said okay. So we went down the stairs to the lower level and it was still dark, I had not even turned on the lights! The bag was still there in the chair just where I said it was. He took the antenna of his walkie-talkie and touch the bag, then he took it back. He then took his antenna again and lifted the bag up about 2 inches from the chair, we heard a sound coming from the bag that made us look at each other with the big eye shock and amazement look! The sound we heard was that of a baby who was in distress! It was a baby crying sound! He told me to go turn on the lights and he grabbed the bag. As lights came on he took the stairs in a swift fashion. I joined him. We had to go back thru the crowded lobby with this bag in our hands and not raise suspicion to anybody that something strange was going on. We somehow managed the endeavor and made it to the emergency room. Out of breath and shaking, I told them what had just happened. They grabbed the bag from security and laid it on the table. It seems that it was a plastic grocery bag and inside that bag was another plastic bag and inside the other bag was a sheet and as they unwrapped the sheet there was a newborn baby boy, placenta with umbilical cord and intact. At that point I started sweating and crying! They had to physically sit me down and take my blood pressure. This was more than I could handle at this time. I was not ready!

Meanwhile other nurses had immediately started an IV on this baby which was located in his head! They transferred him to neonatal intensive care unit where I stood vigil all night until they airlifted him to another hospital. This poor baby had a hematoma on his head so big that they had to transfer him to where they could care for him either he was dropped on his head during the birth procedure or his head was hit as he was tossed on that chair, somehow this baby had a head injury. I started crying all over again. They had to tell me to calm myself down because of the delicate nature of my pregnancy. I followed the story of the baby which I named Little Willie in the media. Before they transferred him, I watched him from the nursery window to the chopper. When it took off I wondered what was going to happen to him. He eventually died three weeks later. As far as me and my nosey self, I got more than what I bargained for that night. I was a hero at the hospital and made the newspaper. It made me appreciate my children even more. Who throws away a kid? They put out police notifications searching for the mother at different places and hospitals but to this day they never found her.

All I remember is looking up from my glass dining room table face down, sprawled across it. As I looked up my eyes caught a glimpse of a glass wine decanter vase I used as a decoration for the center of the table. I grabbed that vase firmly at the neck, came around and went to work with a three piece to his head. On the third blow the vase flew out of my hand and I could not find it. Damn I was not finished! He regains his bearings and the battle was on and intense. He began hitting me with his fist and I was taking those blows and coming back with my own. Bobbing and weaving. Altho my licks rocked him, they were not enough to demobilize him. The first blow was when he hit me hard enough to knock me down and then that abusive bitch jumped on top of me and started choking me. My only thought was that another man will not beat me again without a good fight and that I would be willing graciously to face a 1st degree murder charge, not assault or attempted murder, but murder! Whatever happens I am ready to deal with it. I grabbed between his legs into his prized nutsack and went to work again. I stuck my nails in and gripped a handful and I started twisting and snatching and pushing my nails into them. That got him up off of me. I can remember him saying "Imma kill you bitch! I will kill you!" while he was choking me when he had me. I remember those words were said to me before during another time in my life with men taking advantage of me in a way that I couldn't fight back. Not this time buddy! I'm going down in flames if I have to, but if so, let it burn! This will not happen to me again as I continued the twisting of his prized nutsack to get him up off of me. We continued fighting throwing stuff at each other, tearing up the house we shared. I am telling you, I was not going down easy. I know could not beat him fighting, I wanted him to know that there would be a fight and no backing down and if this is the route he wanna take, let's travel. Every time he thought we were finished fighting and he sat down, I immediately lunged at him again thinking to myself, this nigga hit me and the fight was on again! He then distributed the ending below by hitting me in my right eye so hard that it sent me to the floor. I wore hard contacts at that time so the contact was in my eye when he hit me. I grabbed my face and ran towards the door got into my car and discovered that the battery was no longer there. Yeah that is what started the fight. He tried to take his battery out of my car while I was in it. He loosened the cables and I drove away with the hood up and all! I was so angry I came back to the house, finished taking the battery cables off with my bare hands and threw the battery at him! That's right I threw it at him! I was a mad black woman who was supporting everything at that house and all he had was a raggedy truck that wasn't working and a good car battery! That is all he had and after all these months of living with me, using my stuff and tearing up my stuff you wanna take the only thing you brought to the table? I am so glad my children were gone for the weekend because it would not have been a pretty scene when the police arrived. My daughter would have killed him!. I was there sitting in my car crying remembering everybody is around the corner, It is Thanksgiving, I know they are there. I should just drive around or run around and get my family members then I thought. Bu if they saw my face they will kill him and one of my family members will be in jail for murder.   I can't do that so I'm just sitting in the car crying in shock.   I can't believe after 5 years he actually put his hands on me.   He was the man I made passionate love to.   He was the man that cooked for me and my family.   He was the man that made me laugh in the hardest of times. He was the man i loved! I am just sitting in my unlocked car thinking, how could this happen? Why did this happen? He then comes out of the house looking for me, sees me and proceeds to get in the car with me crying pleading, telling me he is so sorry that this happened, that he loved me and he don't know what happened to him.   He said he would rather kill himself than hurt me.   At that point I was willing to see how far he would go with the threat of killing himself because he was dead to me.   As I looked he had my 22 Derringer pearl handle pistol in his hand, but then he said this to me, "if I can't have you then nobody else will have you" Fumbling with the gun, I'm looking at him in shock.   First of all you said you would rather hurt yourself than hurt me and now you say that you rather nobody else have me.   Make up your mind fool. Which one is it? I just looked at him thinking this shit with my damaged face, blood everywhere, my hair all torn out of my head in spots, my clothes torn off me, feeling like my world has been pushed out of the universe and he talking about he'd rather hurt himself than hurt me. Be my guest buddy! I don't believe you, show me. After what i just experienced   I really wish you would just turn into a piece old dust and blow away right now! Whatever happened, whatever he thought at that moment he got out of my car and with the gun, walked towards the alley.   I'm still sitting in the car wondering where he went through his mind, what he's up to, thinking about what i felt, then I hear my gun go off. I'm thinking to myself I hope this bitch shot himself in the head and nobody finds him! I hope he did not miss! I then get out of my car and go into the house go downstairs get in the bed bloody clothes and all.   I felt like this was a dream. This can't be happening to me, he said he loved me and I cried and I cried. Hours went by, after a while I hear him coming down the stairs, I say to myself "damn he still alive, that sorry asshole did not die!" He comes and lays next to me still saying he's sorry. Still begging my forgiveness. At this point I'm too weak mentally, emotionally and physically, too weak to fight, to speak. Just devastated. Just a shell of a woman. He precedes to climb on top of me and "do his business," like in the scene off the movie, "The Color Purple". I felt nothing. I was just like a weak little girl who felt she had nobody and nothing. I bear the lasting emotional and physical scar of being a victim of domestic violence from the man who said he loved me, being blind in my right eye. I can truly say he loved me blindly.

September 11, 2005 marks another day that changed my life forever. I have a lot of life changing events and this was the day that I became a gunshot victim statistic. Let me tell you how it all happened, my niece and I decided to go out in Omaha and my cousin was going to join us. It was about maybe 11:30 at night and my niece and I just riding down 16th Avenue. We parked the car and got out. We were just out on this lovely night talking to each other, enjoying each other's company while we waited on our other guest to arrive. We decided not to go into the strange-looking club and everybody was outside on their cars and everywhere. It seems like nobody was in the club everybody was outside. Similar to a scene from the movie Dusk to Dawn. After a while about 12:30 a.m. our cousin arrived. She parked her car in front of ours. She told us her phone was dead and asked my niece could she use her phone to call her husband. After she finished talking to her husband she was handing the phone back to my niece. We headed towards her car for some strange reason we stopped for a moment, we don't know what made us stop but we did. Out of nowhere four guys came and stood behind us. We thought that they were admiring how gorgeous we looked or how beautiful we were and the next thing I heard was pop! Pop! Pop! Pop pop! and my niece fell to the ground saying "they shootin'! They shootin'!" the next thing I heard coming from across the street was boom! Boom! Boom boom! The people across the street were shooting back with bigger guns! It appears that the guys behind us opened fire on the guys across the street from us and they will using us as shields! We were caught in the middle of gang or some type of crossfire. All I know is that there were bullets flying everywhere! My niece was already on the ground and I was on the ground with her because I covered her with my body. She was bleeding from her shoulder and as she called 911 with her left thumb and she right handed! She exhibited such courage that I had to stop bleeding and look at her twice in amazement as she talked to the 911 dispatcher. She said "two down, two down!" I looked at her and asked her, "what you five o or something? Who the hell are you, a secret agent or something?" The strange thing is she never answered any of my questions. Meanwhile I start to scramble around looking for my cousin. I managed to find her and she also had been shot, hers was upper thigh. She had on a beautiful pair of white culottes that was saturated in blood and she was still looking beautiful sitting there in shock. I managed to round up both of the girls crawling scrambling around crawling and herding them towards safety between two trucks. All I could think about is my sister gonna kill me and her husband gonna kill me! I am the oldest of the bunch, I should have been more careful where I went with them. Then I noticed that my leg was burning and wet. I thought I had scratched myself on the truck so as I got the girls to a safe place. I placed my hand on the inside of my thigh to see if I had peed on myself. I was really scared so that was the first thought that crossed my mind, you peed on yourself girl. As I removed my hand I noticed it was covered in a red substance my next thought was damn I've been shot! I had on a black dress that require no bra and a pair of Joe Boxer Black and Yellow skimpy underwear as I got between two trucks with the other bleeding family members. The streets have been clear and very quiet, then all of a sudden like in The Wizard of Oz when the house fell on the witch, all the people start coming out mumbling and looking. A guy came running across the street with a light cell phone shining it on us, asking about is anybody hurt, is everybody alright. We said "yeah everybody okay over here" because we did not know who was shooting at us and we did not know if he was coming to finish the job of making us dead. Yeah we all are ok! Now back to me and the blood running down the bullet hole in my leg. People who have hiding were coming out from between buildings and under cars and stuff. I told the people who were gathering around us, "I'm sorry what you about to see is nothing but black ass because I got shot and I need to see where I'm shot at!" As I raised my dress up we heard a clinking sound and everybody looked at everybody. The bullet had went completely all the way through my thigh and it was all crumpled up like a piece of paper. It fell out of me! It went clean thru my damn leg!

We hear ambulances sirens coming from afar and my cousin is still sitting there in shock looking beautiful. How can a gunshot victim look so pretty and injured at the same time? They loaded my niece into one ambulance and they loaded me and my cousin into another ambulance together. She was not cooperative at all and I was overly cooperative. Once again I want to know if I have been shot anywhere else. I was laying on the stretcher and I grabbed the bottom of my dress and raised it over my head. I asked the paramedic "do you see any other bullet holes in me?" Their faces were flushed so red that I don't know if they looked of European descent anymore. They kinda looked pale faced or pasty! Meanwhile on the next stretcher my cousin is telling the paramedics "don't touch me!" while they're cutting off her brand new white blood stained culottes. Seems they were not listening. The ambulance begins to proceed toward the hospital and I look out the window as we're passing the car that my niece and I were getting ready to get into but stalled for a few minutes and then got shot before we made it. That little pink car was full of bullet holes and if we had gotten into that car I would not have been here to tell you this story. When we arrived at the hospital and got situated the police came into the room, it was two of them with a camera wanting to take pictures of my gunshot wound. Once again I had to raise up my dress and show my black ass and my yellow with black Joe Boxer thongs that said Queen. Since they wanted to take pictures I gave them a view that left their faces the exact same color red as the paramedics. That was another strange thing in the strangest thing of that strange night. Why was all their faces turning beet red when I showed them the entrance and exit wound site? All I did was laid on my side or either on my back and raised my right leg up so they could get a good accurate picture, what was wrong with that? What made all their faces so red at different times? I had been shot and traumatized. They wanted to see, I showed them the same exact spot!.,

Now back to me bleeding to death mentally. The bullet went straight through my thighs and exited close to my butt. I did not get shot in the butt! I got shot in my upper thigh for the record, not in my ass. The 40 caliber bullet did not hit my femoral artery thankfully. They dosed me up with morphine and sent me home with crutches. My nephew who ha been out came to get me and my courageous niece, told me later that the Morphine was working cause I talked all the way home. Thank God for him being there for us. We needed to see his handsome face. We made the news and the newspapers, name age and all. We were informed by the Victim Assistance Unit after the shooting that the police found 52 bullet casings on the ground after that shooting 53 with the one that fell from my wound. I came to the realization that either they were bad shots or what I know to be true is that God protected me and my family. All I knew it that I was alive!

The road to recovery was quite the trip, first of all I had to keep telling people that I did not get shot in my ass, I got shot in my upper right thigh. Close but no cigar.

My physical therapy everyday was walking to my niece house to see how she was recuperating and to help her with her household duties because she could not use her arm. My cousin was okay, she was wounded but she could function and she had a husband who was there for her.

Informing the family and friends of the Incident was the hardest, everybody was in amazement that I had left the Murder Capital. Gary IN where I had survived without a scratch to go to "The Good Life" Omaha NE to get shot. This is the Cornhusker state, they were supposed to be throwing corn cobs at me, not shooting bullets!

This story right here got to be shared! What a morning! I'm up about 6 am letting my dog outside. Her name was Beauty. She was strange pitbull she had one green and one blue eye and her coat was pure white. Back to the story, I had a large 3 story house with a large open porch. When the dog went outside she went to the end of porch to get into her cage. I'm following her outside in my nightgown with a couple coffee in my hand. Usually the street is empty at this time of morning but this particular morning that was a car, a silver Ford focus with six white guys and brown jacket and khaki pants standing around the vehicle. I quickly felt the need to turn around and go in to the house, first of all because I had no clothes on and second of all whatever my neighbors did I did not want to know about it. I kicked that door so fast and turned damn near running into the house. Then I hear Bam! Bam! Bam! "Open the door! This is Omaha Police Department!" I asked the police, "Why? Ain't nobody in here did nothing!" The police responded "We want to talk to you!" My response "About what?" His response was "About the two dead bodies in the car in front of your house!" Now you know I wouldn't about the action of opening that door! I ran downstairs to where my son was and told him what was going on upstairs and outside. He came upstairs with me and we opened the door and went outside together where the police were standing on the porch. It appears that there was a man and a woman in the car. The man had been shot at least 7 times, he on the passenger side. The driver who was female was shot in the head execution style. I never saw the bodies, I didn't want to see them and didn't care to see them. I did not know these people! The strangest thing of all is about 1 a.m. I heard what I thought was firecrackers and the reason is because that were firecrackers on my front porch. I told my younger cousin earlier not to light them. I figured he lit them anyway and I was going to handle that situation in the morning. So I went back to sleep. Those were the gunshots that will being fired in that car in front of my house that I heard. Thank God I went back to bed and did not go out there fussing at my cousin.

Meanwhile let's go back to the part of the story with the police are at my house. My son and I began to communicate with the police and ask them what was going on they told us that there were two dead bodies in front of the house and no suspect. They say that they have been there since 1:30 a.m. investigating the crime scene which meant they ran my plates on my van, they rummaged through my garbage, ran a background check on me and every adult in the house because they asked me, " This is quite different from Gary Indiana isn't it?" They have been out there while investigating me and my household I guess, after all it was it was a murder scene. They said that they were waiting on the coroner to get there, mind you this is about 7:30 am now. Wow! I had children that were going to daycare and how was I supposed to get them past two dead bodies in the car in front of the house that surrounded with yellow tape. I asked the police "How am I supposed to keep my children past this violent scene?" so they offered me this solution that my boys come out the back door and someone's walk them down the street and inform the daycare driver that's where they'll pick him up. My older grandson was tall enough to shield them from what was behind them as he walked them down the street. okay I got them out of that one I have now gotten dressed and is on the porch watching the crime scene. All kind of police cars and news cameras have arrived now. Oh by the way did I tell you I have only been in that house for 7 days? I just moved into the neighborhood!

It is now about 9:30am and the bodies are still in front of the house in the car! The coroner eventually got there and they set up a black shield that you cannot see over above under or through and they began to remove the bodies from the car. The news team made it to me and begin to question me about the situation I told him that I had been there only one week and so far this Fair City has been very interesting to me. This was one of the times I began to questions my moving to Omaha, but behind every cloud there's a silver lining. The news reporter that interviewed talked after the interview. I told him of my journey of working with parents and families. He told me about the organization he was working and that there was a small window and that they may be interested in my journey parental involvement and engagement. They were the African American Achievement Council, a group of wonderful people who were working toward bridging the cultural achievement gap. As the time went by, they assisted and partnered with me with Parents School Community involvement and engagement His wife and I will always joke about how many times I called him about meeting with him, she would tell people in a laughing way she believed that I was stalking her husband. She probably was right. I was on an educational mission She and I and became members of the district and community, we got to be a great team. We made good things happen in different capacities. All I know that in life everything that happens for a reason. Nothing is really happenstance and I know this.

Chapter 8. Dating and Relationships

The bodyguards do what the bodyguards do!

Chapter 8. Dating and Relationships.

Dating with 6 males in the house was not an easy task for me or the person that I intend to share a possible romantic interest with. It seems like I'm the queen in the high castle and the person the king or whoever supposed to rescue me must have all kinds of gadgets and weapons and everything to get possibly to the edge of the moat under the keen watchful eye of the guards. So far no survivors. I have had some great challengers but not survivors. They even liked some of them too.

I chose not to date or put any man through this type of intimidating situation because I knew sooner or later they would grow up and leave the nest or find some interest that requires them to get out of my business. If I could just manage to get them to a point in their lives where I could begin my social life as I would have it things would be cool. Not so! What is it about boys as they get older and live in the same with you they get worse? They become more protective, more observant, more critical just more everything toward momma. There were points were I had to put Crazy Action Plan #60 in play by telling that young person who lost his mind in my household by trying to me what to wear, what to say, where I can and cannot go, "Shid you don't like the situation, there is the door. I will miss you. Need some help?" That really helps when he gets a case of him smelling himself in my business.

Another reason why dating with the boys around was so hard for me was because they had experienced first time seeing their mom abused, seeing their mom cry over relationships, just seeing that Mama was hurt disappointed and lost over men. Whether they verbalized it or not it shows up in their actions when they were younger they felt that they needed to do something and was helpless. As they got older, they do, they watch mama cry, vent and however else she expresses herself, they want to protect her and sometimes they're a little overprotective or even aggressive but that's their way of saying, "Mama I got you this time."

One of the things that I never got a chance to show my boys was the effects of a male-female relationship for a long period of time because I never had a stable relationship to show them how they were supposed to treat their woman or give them examples. I didn't like that. I felt I should have done better in the relationship department as far as showing them how things are done in relationships when dating, and sharing and spending time with women. I guess you could say I may have been selfish in that aspect of life. The true supporting evidence to that statement is somewhere in the stratosphere, I really don't know.

I'm reflecting on every time I thought I had a nice man to bring to bring home to meet my boys, something would go wrong after they meet him. You know the normal relationship break up stuff like they were married, got married, got kids somewhere, unfaithful, cheater, don't have a job, on drugs, goes to jail, wants to be abusive, you know the normal stuff and that ends relationships and here I am once again stuck looking like a desperate woman accepting any kind of behavior towards me from men. "I am not going to look like that again!" I said to myself. My fellas are not going to see me in a vulnerable state self pity and devastation.

As far as the fellas dating and bringing ladies into my home, that is a whole nother book. This is a subject in my home that has caused a lot of problems. I have rules and standards. Sometimes they learn the good way and sometimes they experience the not so good way. She gonna learn someway today.   You see i try real hard to be nice to some of the women who visit our home, the one thing that i really observe is how she acts in my home the minute she enters my door. Does she speak? How does she introduce herself? How is her hygiene? Does she make herself too comfortable? Is she respectful with her mouth? Her actions activate my top notch reaction center. How she acts in my presence is how she will vet treated in my presence, with a few exceptions by me. I can zip up a clown suit with big red shoes included or i can wear my shiny halo and smile. It is truly up to her and how she treats me. It is called understanding.

Chapter 9. My Friends

Ain't Nobody like them.

Chapter 9. My friends

Now I must talk about my friends I called them my earthly angels because in some way or another they had been an angel to put up with some of my crazy madness as a friend. I'm a piece of work and so are they. We love, know, understand and recognize that fact   Each friend has a different role in my life and I value and respect them dearly.

I have a friend that would have heated debates with me to the point what people thought we were going to fight. Then afterwards we would go have a meal, have a drink or a casino creep. We could be mad as hell with each other behind closed doors, screaming at each other, but when we emerge from that room, on whatever enclosed area we need to talk by ourselves, we come out in a unified front. No one will ever know what happened in that room between us but us unless you at standing at the door and hear the exchange of words, furniture crashing, glass breaking, chairs and tables being tossed or pounded on. But when that door opens we come out like we the best of friends, like we just did not have a knock-down, drag out episode in that room. I dunno what you heard or who you heard standing at the door, but that wasn't us. Nope.

I have friends that are level headed calm cool and collected very well-educated Everyday People.   These angels are no joke. I thank God for them and I appreciate them and sometimes I wonder if I am the kind of friend to them that they are to me. I am thankful of all the years we shared, all the dreams we talked about and all the goals we achieved. How did they put up with me? I could share so many stories of how I got crazy and they managed to put up with me and pulled me through stupid situations wondering what was I thinking. I'm glad I had earthly angels at my side. There are so many stories that I cannot tell them all or I might miss someone so I will just cite a few of our wonderful moments. See if you remember the time when:

You stopped me from creating a race riot on 61st and Broadway when the white lady stopped us and turn told us "I hope all you black people just drop dead!" Your spirituality, level- headedness and your personality help me realized that I have would have been making a serious mistake by beating that lady up like I wanted to. You have tried to help me keep my spirituality intact, however there were times I thought you would just throw in the friendship towel but you didn't. You and your beautiful God fearing God loving family have been my help and my strength. Thanks for sticking around even when I woulda left.

You called the police on me because you wanted to save my life and or me going to prison for murder because I had an abusive boyfriend and you witnessed an incident where I was fed up and overwhelmed. You were scared for me, you were not afraid that I was going to get beat up, but you were afraid of what I did and what I was going to continue to do upside his head with that iron skillet. I could not have been mad at you because you have been there for the last 30 + years in my life so I trusted and trust your judgement. Good looking out. Also you were there almost everyday that my daughter was at home ill. You held me up so many days I thought I could not make it through.

How about the time I watched you complete your bachelor's degree and graduate from one of the top colleges in the country with your Juris Doctorate. You made me realize that there is nothing that I could not do if I put my mind to it. You taught me what a real friendship is all about also. I want to thank you for loving me enough to cut your vacation short when I lost my daughter. You have stood by me through thick and thin and some happy hectic and hard times. You contributed to me appreciating and valuing my sense of worth. You are a true friend indeed.

You were there when I experience my second house fire. I was unable mentally and physically to respond to the situation, you stepped up and stepped in without a second thought. You were and are a real trooper. You got my stuff from across the street from the burnt house with it still smoky and smoldering and brought it to my office and set it up all by yourself. I could not have made it through that situation without you. I looked at you in amazement as I watched you walk down the street carrying my belongings with one boot and one shoe on your feet. You have been strength and muscle that I need and needed in hard times. If that ever happened to be an apocalypse I would definitely want you on my team. You are truly my Macgyver.

I cannot believe that after all these years of being friends all of this time that we have been diagnosed with the exact same autoimmune disease we have been neighbor for a long time who shared a lot of conversations you are one of my married friends and you have taught me what true love is about and how marriage supposed to work you have taught me how to be laid back and not worry a lot your calming personality certainly saved my son's life that day. You caught me speeding down 8th Avenue and stopped me, asked me where I was going so fast. I told you I was headed to the school to beat the breaks off my son. You began to talk to me. I needed that calmness and level-headedness at the exact time we turned the corner in opposite directions. We both have experienced the loss of our first born child and so many other life experiences. So glad we're neighbors and wherever I live you will forever be my Neighbor.

You are the friend whose taste in shoes, clothes and jewelry I adore. You brought me into bright colors and told me to stop hiding myself in those "browns" because those bright colors bring out your beautiful skin tone and your beauty. Because you are creative and very talented woman in so many aspects of life I value your opinion and fashion savvy. Yep you are the wardrobe consultant every woman needs and wants. You made me believe in me when I thought I was failing so many times I wanted to give up but your bright smile and your courage two-faced whatever gave me courage to face whatever you've driven many miles to come get me and I'll make sure that I was safe in okay without asking me for one dime. No matter where this life takes us, your friendship to me is priceless..

You always said "Willie Williams, Imma need you to get it together!" whenever I was slipping and trying to have a pity party. I got it together too! We started working with families together and you really believed in me and we spent a great deal of time putting things together and making things work for families. We had several other personal adventures that we shared with and without our children. You were so well groomed, manicured and pedicured that you got me a lot more in to this part of my life again. I always commented on how they looked. We will always be friends

We met at an organizing table and found out we share the same birthday. That started a wonderful friendship and working relationship. We have organized some fantastic community events. It is always great to work beside you because I know whatever we do we gonna get it done well. You are that dependable person that knows everybody and enjoys people. Your smile and your different hairstyles makes you so unique my business community birthday partner to the end. I can count on you when the chips are down and somehow you find a way to make things positive.

I was sitting beside you for two years playing, laughing, winning on the buffalo slot machine. I used to look for you because we had fun when we got together. Never once did it cross my mind that you would be part of the family in Omaha I was given my marching orders to find. When I left Gary he said, "Esther Mae Jean when you get to Omaha, find my daddy!" We laughed. He gave me his father's name again and told me to "get busy". It took me a minute as a matter of fact it took two years to "get busy"

It was so coincidental that I was talking to a real good friend I met in Omaha years ago. I spent a lot of time with her and we shared a lot of great hours at the bid whist table. We were just having one of our talks and I mentioned the conversation I had with my friend about finding his dad. She asked me the father's name. I told her. She said "I know him! Wait a minute." Then she began to make some calls. She gave me the phone after dialing and talking to the last phone number, informing me it the dad I was looking for! I took the phone and asked the gentleman some questions to make sure it was the right person and it was! I asked him if I could give his number to his son, he said yes. I called the young man and asked him, " What did you tell me to do?" He said "Find my father who I never met. I am 40 years old and ain't never met him!" I said "Well get a pen and paper and write this number down so you can call him!" He did. He called me back crying saying "Thank you Esther Mae Jean. You found my daddy! I finally get to meet him!" They met in person as father and son in Omaha with his side of the family hosting a welcoming, well attended, loving feast for the newest family member and his family. I was there at the party too. It was so good seeing and experiencing the love that was shown to my friend firsthand. I met the dad who was an attractive, well groomed, well dressed older man that smelled so good! When we were introduced he immediately took my hand, looked me in my eyes and said to me, "You are my angel, thank you" And smiled ever so sweetly to the point I felt the love and the appreciation he was expressing. The door opens as we were finishing our conversation and in walks my friend who I had been sharing casino time with playing the buffalo's! She was my friend's daddy's sister! The person who was right next to me all this time was who I needed to ask and I didn't! We just looked at each other and laughed. I was in awe! God put the answer right there and I was busy trying to find it by no looking at the obvious. God really got a sense of humor. Time went on and my friend and his father enjoyed each other's company and the two families got to know more about each other. Suddenly my friend's father died. Then a year or so later my friend died. I am so thankful that they got to meet each other on earth, now they can walk around heaven together too.

All my friends are very important and special to me. They know i got issues and they still like me. I've had some real friendship that have lasted over 40 years. These friendships have impacted my life in a fashion I love. I would like to thank the nurses on 4 West nursing unit, Methodist Hospital, Gary, IN. The people who took time to mentor a 19 year single mom who was entering the grown up workforce for the very first time. I ain't saying it was all peaches, bananas and cream, it was truly a loving and learning experience. You wonderful women in white and in blue on that unit, you strong dedicated soldiers for health taught me about life, friendship, work ethics and some much more. I cherish memories and the time spent. Remember, there wasn't no party like a 4 West Christmas party! We were a team of healthcare professionals who rocked on and off the unit.

Chapter 10. Them

Men are such real blessings or such real lessons.

Chapter 10. Them

This chapter is taking a small peek at some of the experiences with men in my life. Some good, some not so good and some downright terrible but never the less they are my experiences.

Me and the ladies were out on a nice summer night looking for something to do, we heard about a dance at the pavillion so we decided to go check it out. The crowd was not what we expected so we got back in the car and as we were sitting there a car that pulled up beside us and parked. A carload of fellows! It was 5 of us and 5 of them! Wow! I was still feeling a little uncertainabout myself because my self-esteem and everything and I was wearing my glasses. Nobody ever talks to me with these thick ass glasses on. I am going to be the girl left sitting in the car again.

So the guys got out the car and came over to the car and started choosing the girls in the car to talk to and I was in the back seat quiet trying to be invisible so i won't have to experience rejection again.   The tallest finest of the carload of handsome, well groomed brothers came over to the side where I was, looked in the car and asked me to get out. Me being not that confident and a little shaky not knowing what to expect, I got out the car. I have to admit I was looking delicious that night. I have a nice button turquoise plaid down shirt shirt and a swell pair of jeans that were fitting every curve that I owned, a pair of tall heels and my hair cut short and curly. As I got out the car and stood up, he came over to me and gave me one simple command, "turn around", he said. So I did a complete circle for him to observe every curve those jeans were hugging. Next he said "now take off take off those glasses let me see your eyes" I did. The way he looked at me as I stood there was not a way I had ever been looked at before. It was just different. He looked at me in a way that made me feel like I was the prize. His eyes said it all. That moment on that night under that moonlight in that parking lot was the night I fell in love was a tall dark handsome real life United States soldier. His smile was a killer too!

We began to share each other's company and I would feel butterflies in my stomach whenever he came anywhere near me. The passion and the lust I felt for this man was insatiable and he responded in the same manner, we enjoyed each other. He got stationed out of the country and things on top of things happened. He came back stateside we were still into each other. I loved the ground this man walked on. He was truly my first love. He made me feel desired and sexy. I actually lived the emotions so sought after in love songs. I experienced love and then he got married but not to me.

I was new to the city didn't know anyone but family and I was trying to fit in. I spent a lot of time with family at sporting events. My son played basketball for the local high school and was the star player, so a lot of people came to see him play. This particular night I was in the stands and my nephew and his friends who are also his fraternity brothers. They are sitting about 5 benches ahead of me. They were a group of handsome, sexy, smart brothers and they were slowly leaving the game one by one before it was over. As one of then was leaving he was climbing up the bleachers he used my shoulder as a way to steady himself. He was so cute and intriguing somehow between him touching my shoulder and departing for the door he gave me his card with all his numbers on it. Not only did he give me is card, but as his hand touched me I got a smooth chill. Don't ask me to explain the feeling cause I can't. I could not wait to get home to call him. He was unavailable forthe for the first few numbers that I called but then he called me back. We had a delightful conversation. We were just talking about anything and everything just a good conversation and then I asked him two dreaded question, How old are you?" he said "24" and I dropped the phone! I was 23 years his senior and he was hanging in there with conversation that made me thought he was around my age. I picked the phone backup and ask him what am I supposed to do with you and his comment was "Anything you want to do." Damn he did not understand I have not been with a man in a long time and this youngster was asking for serious trouble. Hmmmm. Well my curiosity about him got the best of me, he was a young tender, but yet he was so old and that he was quite fascinating to me. We hooked up to go out on a first date on New Year's Eve. I tried to break the date and he held my feet to the fire so I had to woman up. We went on that date and we had fun, a whole lot of fun and that's the night he made me realize that age is nothing but a number. After that we had several dates and lustful rendezvous. He took my adventurous side and turned it on. He was that spark that I needed in that moment of time and space. Most of all he made me feel young, sexy, desirable and beautiful. Hell he made me a believer out of me. Impressive.

I could say he were just a waste of my time and I didn't even realize it, but I was so excited by his different nature and his crazy antics that I did not see clearly that he was a little challenged. May be not but he did roll to his own drum beat no matter who liked it or not. He is his truly one of a kind and I liked his craziness, at least some of it. I really did enjoy being around him at times, because besides being a psycho, he did take good care of me in all areas. He made me laugh. He read to me. We had day parties. We did have fun with each until one of his many going off the rails episodes. One thing for sure he reinforced to me that there is a thin line between love and hate. No he was not a waste of my time, he was a lesson that taught me well. He taught me that you can be smart crazy, that is when you smart as hell but crazy as a road lizard! Thanks for the ride.

It was during the hardest time of my life that I was finally coming out and socializing with people I was walking down Broadway in Gary Indiana when I heard someone yell "Hey Willie!" I turned around and it happened to be one of my old friends that I haven't seen in a while. So as you know I was just trying to live after the death of my daughter. This gentleman and I have had a past so it was good to see him we exchange numbers again. We started going out and little did I know that he was just as heartbroken as I was because he had lost custody of his children due to a problem that was not his own. I had lost my daughter and he his children, we held each other on many nights and cried together. I would always tell him that he could be able someday to touch his children but I would never be able to touch my daughter again. He would just hold me some nights and some nights I would just hold him two. We were two injured souls lost in the night due to the loss of our children in one way or the other. We formed a bond.

We began to live together and things were okay. I just was not good after my daughter's death, so he just couldn't reach me the way he wanted to and I could not open up the way I needed to, nevertheless he tried. One day I told him I wanted to visit my brother in Omaha. He drove me and my boys to Omaha to visit for about a week. Little did he know I was not going to come back to Gary because it was so painful and I was with my brother who I was always with thru hard times. So I relocated to Omaha without telling him. He tells me that I am still his girlfriend because we did not break up, I moved. Yes I still love him.

My Victory Laps

To those guys who in my senior year of high school took for me the only thing that I could call my own.   You beat me violently and then you took my person. For a long time that person was so low as a young woman that she went through so many trials and tribulations trying to find herself or trying to make herself feel better within her spirit.   It was not until she found herself stronger wiser and better, she realized that this horrible situation was not her fault. You three guys were cowards and wanted to be big men but the actions you took against a virgin was totally a piece of shit move. You watched me grow up and then you did this despicable act to me.   I have never fully recovered mentally and emotionally from this situation. I deal with the trauma associated with being a rape victim. There are times as an adult woman I go into defense mode when I feel like I am helpless in circumstances and the outcome is never pretty. I don't like being in large crowds especially the ones where there are a lot of men in the crowd. I still have residual effects. What I want you sack of shit piece of men to know that you may have won the battle, however I won the war. I am still standing strong. I am successful and I am helping other women have a voice. I have had raised my family and they are productive men in society unlike you itty bitty boys who feel they have to take women forcibly to feel big. The men in my life will not let something this terrible happen to me without serious consequences and repercussions. I am confident of that!

Now for you Mr Pastor man. Does the church know in July 1977 that you took a 19 year old girl into the woods in Dyer Indiana to attack her, tear her clothes off of her because I did not want to have sex with you? Did you tell your congregation that you were drunk and scary? Did you tell them you threatened to put me out of the car in the middle of a dark street because I asked you, "Where are we going?" and you said "To make love!" I said "Not to me you're not!!" and then you said "Get Out!" I said "Ok I will!" You looked at me like a drunken sly fox and then put your foot to the gas pedal and floored it. You worked for EJ&E Railroad so you knew this area well. As we were driving through the backwoods we passed one car. You drove so far into that wooded area where there was nothing but tall trees, parked and the fight began in the front seat of your car. Not again in less than 18 months I was fighting for my person! This time whoever raped me was going to rape a dead body because I was not that same girl! I meant that shit! He was gonna have to kill me to get this!

I was dressed in all my new clothes because it was the fourth of July and you asked me to ride to Chicago Il to take your godmother home. You had always been a gentleman and now you are a monster. You grabbed my blouse and asked me, "Do you like this blouse?' With tears in my eye and shaking, all I could do was nod. The look in your eyes was terrifying! You grabbed the waistline of my new black gauchos and started to pull them and I was pulling back! He ripped the zipper! I was still fighting hard for my person. I was losing and I fell back on the seat, covered my eyes and said "Lord have mercy, Lord have mercy, Lord have mercy!" He stopped pulling at my clothes all of a sudden, when I opened my eyes there was a police car with lights flashing and the officer was at the car window trying to open the door! It seems like the one car we passed was a police woman and in the 70's Blacks were not supposed to be in that area. Thank God for being black in the 70's! I got out of the car holding my clothes and crying. The officer asked me did I want to go with him or stay with this would be rapist? I jumped in the back seat of that police car so fast you thought I was under arrest! As the officer was driving to the station he told me the last girl they found in these woods were eaten by the animals that it was hard to identify her. I just wonder would he have killed me or left me in those woods? God said no! Does the congregation know that there was a police report filed on their maniac pastor for assault?

I will never date another married man ever in my life because it is the worst feeling in the world when you get that shit back! Karma ain't got no friends! His wife was my friend and I let lust, curiosity and plain selfishness get the best of me and it destroyed our friendship. I loved his children but I couldn't stop! I hurt them too. He was their loving dad at home with their mom being a family and here I was. I did fall in love with him to a point where I thought that I could and would not be able to live without his touch, boy was I a sick fool! This relationship went on for so many years to the place where I destroyed some many relationships because he was always there when I needed him, when my world would be falling down he was always willing to pick me up, do whatever it took to make me feel better. Whatever I needed and wanted. I was the cause of my world falling apart because all I had to do was let go, but I couldn't. I was the problem and did not care! I was so weak for him! This man was truly my kryptonite. All he had to do was smile, touch me and all the fight and good reasoning was gone. My clothes would come off by themselves! I can truly say I was dick whipped to a point of foolishness. It took for him to do me like I did his wife for me to feel the effect of the damage I had done to my life. I should have left him alone a long time ago and maybe I would have stayed married, had a real relationship or had a new husband to share my life. I couldn't, he was like a drug. One thing for sure I will not do a married man again because this one got married again and it wasn't me. I really thought it would be but it wasn't. A wise woman once told me some real shit about when this man and his wife finally broke up and I was excited knowing I would be his next choice. But when I found myself crushed and hurt, I went crying to her. She said to me only as a true friend that don't hold back words would " You a dumb bitch! I told you he looking for a new wife. He going to leave you in girlfriend status cause that is the position you put yourself in and stayed there through all the bullshit, thinking very little of yourself! He wasn't gonna marry you! You were his fun. Now look at you!" Those words stabbed me so hard! She was right. She and I had talked some many times about this relationship and how I was shooting myself in the foot. I did not believe that garbage, he said he loved me and I believed him wholeheartedly. Just as sure as she said it he did it. He broke me all the way down.   The way I broke his family and people who loved me down, but I was broke all the way down under. I was so low an ant's ankle was taller than me. The truth is what goes around comes back around. I felt the effects of my behavior full throttle and I learned that Karma has no friends. The killing insane part is that he was a big part of my life, he was in and out my life,   my life was as open book to him. I loved him with a passion. We made so many beautiful memories. We made such great love. I was so addicted to him, I craved him. I felt I could not live without him, his touch or those long soulful knee shaking kisses. This here sister was sprung! In the end he showed me differently. I was not his favorite choice as a matter of fact I wasn't even in nothing but his bed. Why Shouldn't I have seen that coming? After all those years? Why couldn't I shake him?   The answer was so simple, he messed around on his wife, why was I so different? All I know is if you say you married, I run away real fast. Not ever again.

CONCLUSION

Well I guess that's all I'm writing for now but I thoroughly enjoyed writing and sharing myself with you. I hope you enjoyed reading it because there was sometimes when this book was touch and go. There were times when I put it down and did not pick it backup for quite a while, then out of nowhere someone would say to me, "How's your book coming along or are you almost finished with your book?" So here now that you have read the finished product, I want you to realize that writing about these few pieces of my life in the vast majority of life's test of my ability to survive, I healed. It was a rewarding experience to put my thoughts and words on paper. I might add it was quite an accomplishment.

My book was also designed to give parents or someone raising children somewhere some encouragement. It is to let them know that they are not alone in their journey of life. To know that someone else went through or is going through the same or somebody did the same thing that you do or did. There is light at the end of the tunnel! We are not perfect, we make mistakes as parents.

WARNING: This parenting stuff has no written set of rules. Caution is advised when administering rules after they reach age 10.

Possible Side effects: Episodes of wanting to destroy or kill them, moments of uncontrollable voice volume, may cause moments of self-medication, abandonment for short periods of time and may cause the need for adults to have adult supervision.

I was inspired so much from sharing my story and finally being able to move past what I went through in my life, that I wrote an accompanying interactive workshop series entitled "My Son, My Sun" . This workshop series takes a look at black mother - son relationships and how they communicate. How they think and react on topics presented at a workshop setting. This is a positive, peaceful, productive communication series that is a lot of fun! It also gives mothers and sons another look at their relationship from a different perspective. It really can be tailored to any culture.

So if I go on top of the highest mountain and scream or if I dance in the rain and don't care who watching or simply live each day as if i is my last. If I feel like I have been favored by God, Why Shouldn't I? I have paid some hella dues and I am still standing strong. Peace.

In Loving Memory Of Our Warrior Women!

Sharleece Eshell Curtis
12/1976-01/2004

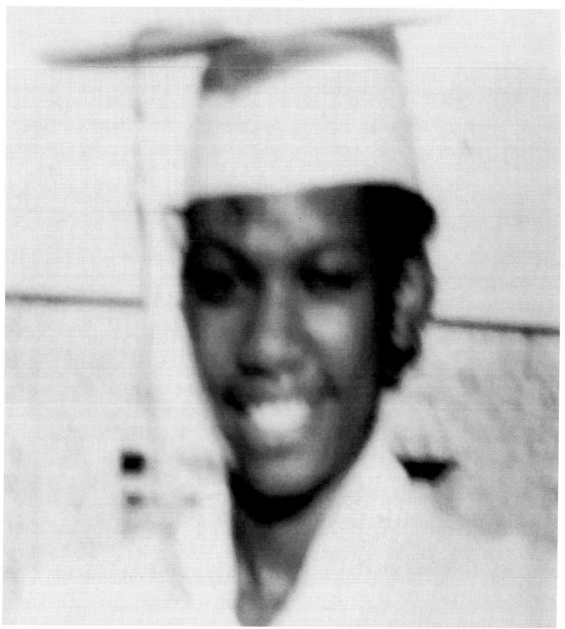

Terri LeeKnight Burtton
05/1977-07/2017

Tyna Fields
08/1975-07/2016

Missing: Still Searching for You My Brother!!

Anthony Roscoe Curtis
3/10/1959

And The Reasons Why I Wrote This Book……..

My Legacy

To them with all my love

Ms. Willie William's Favorite Quote:

"IF YOU ARE A PARENT, RECOGNIZE THAT THIS IS THE MOST IMPORTANT CALLING AND REWARDING CHALLENGE YOU HAVE. WHAT YOU DO EVERY DAY, WHAT YOU SAY AND HOW YOU ACT WILL DO MORE TO SHAPE THE FUTURE OF AMERICA THAN ANY OTHER FACTOR"

MARIAN WRIGHT EDELMAN 1918-

CHILDREN'S DEFENSE FUND OFFICIAL

Made in the USA
Columbia, SC
07 December 2024

47771140R00067